lets be just friends

Camilla is an engineer turned writer after she quit her job to follow her husband in an adventure abroad.

She's a cat lover, coffee addict, and shoe hoarder. Besides writing, she loves reading—duh!—cooking, watching bad TV, and going to the movies—popcorn, please. She's a bit of a foodie, nothing too serious.

A keen traveler, Camilla knows mosquitoes play a role in the ecosystem, and she doesn't want to starve all those frog princes out there, but she could really live without them.

Also by Camilla Isley

__Romantic Comedies__

__Stand Alones__
I Wish for You
A Sudden Crush

__First Comes Love Series__
Love Connection
I Have Never

__New Adult College Romance__

__Just Friends Series__
Let's Be Just Friends
Friend Zone
My Best Friend's Boyfriend

let's be just friends

A New Adult College Romance

Just Friends Series Book 1

CAMILLA ISLEY

This is a work of fiction. Names, characters, businesses, places, events and incidents either are products of the author's imagination or are used fictitiously. Any resemblance to actual events or locales or persons, living or dead, is entirely coincidental.

Dedication

To best friends

One

Rose

Something woke Rose with a start. She tried to pinpoint the source of the noise, but it stopped before she could. A quick peek at the alarm clock sitting in silence on her bedside table told Rose it was only 9:00 a.m. *Good. At least two more hours to sleep.*

The noise started again just as Rose was beginning to drift off. Already half-awake, she managed to identify the sound clearly this time. It was Tyler's phone ringing in the distance. *But, where?* Not in the adjoining room where Rose assumed he was sleeping. No, the sound seemed to be coming from farther away, somewhere on the lower floor of Tyler's townhouse.

Curled under her soft covers, Rose waited for the sound of his quick footsteps down the stairs, but it never came. He must've been fast asleep, in which case she doubted the faint noise of his ringtone would be enough to wake him. Tyler was a heavy sleeper ordinarily, and he'd been out all night, or at least until three this morning when she'd gotten in. She guessed he wouldn't wake up until at least noon.

Rose waited for the phone to stop ringing so she could go back to sleep. But Tyler's vintage MC Hammer ringtone started playing again almost immediately. *Can't touch this...*

Throwing the blankets away from her, Rose sat up and swung her legs off the side of the bed. What the hell! Who was so eager to talk to Tyler this early on a Saturday morning?

Georgiana! The name popped into Rose's mind. She was the only person who'd obsessively binge-call him on a Saturday morning and not get the message people wanted to sleep. Even Tyler's mom would've given up after two missed calls. Why was Georgiana so desperate to talk to him? Did they have a huge fight? Did he finally ditch her? No, that would be too good to be true; they probably just had some kind of argument.

Rose sat on the edge of her bed, tense, listening. The phone had gone quiet again. She waited to hear if it was going to ring again and began twisting her long brown hair into a side braid. Sure enough, after a few seconds, she heard the same familiar tune. *Can't touch this...*

Irritated, she hopped off her bed, threw open her door, and stepped out onto the landing.

Tyler's door was shut. Rose pressed her right ear to the wooden panels. She heard the faint, regular breathing of someone sleeping. Listening more closely, she tried to make out the sound of a second person breathing, but she could only hear Tyler. It seemed he was alone.

Rose stepped away from the door, disappointed. So the argument had not been about Tyler cheating on Georgiana with some other girl. Rose was surprised—and a little annoyed—that Tyler had been faithful to Georgiana for as long as he had. Not that she supported the cheating, but she was eager for Georgiana to be out of their lives, and Tyler *had* cheated on every girl he'd ever been with. It was maddening that the one girl he'd decided to be faithful to was an obnoxious Regina George type.

The house fell silent again. Standing there in the hall in nothing but a turquoise tank top with a frilly trim and matching shorts, Rose shivered. Boston always seemed too cold compared to Texas, no matter the season. She would've preferred to wear an oversized sweater to bed, but last night she'd had no other choices. Busy with her Summer Academic Fellowship for Harvard Law, she hadn't bothered to do laundry in weeks. Her Victoria's Secret PINK set was the only clean thing left at the bottom of the sleepwear drawer. It was either that or two drops of Chanel number five.

Rose massaged her arms with her hands to warm herself up as she turned around, away from Tyler's door and toward the bathroom. *Might as well, since I'm already up.* She finished her business and was about to exit the bathroom when she caught herself in the mirror. Her mini-pajama fit her well. Yes, not bad at all. Pity she turned into a popsicle when she wore them.

Rose moved her gaze up to her face. Her eyes were such a dark brown as to be almost black, and her skin tone made her look constantly tanned. Not like Georgiana with her impossibly white skin, long licorice-black hair, and startling blue eyes. Did Tyler prefer blue eyes? Over the years, he hadn't shown any particular trend in his women. Tall, short, curvy, androgynous, brunette, blonde, redhead—it didn't matter to him. As long as they were attractive.

Tyler's phone began ringing again downstairs. Like an angry cat, Rose hissed at the mirror. How was she supposed to sleep if that damn thing was going to go off every five minutes? She exited the bathroom and ran down the stairs, the carpet muffling her steps.

After a quick scan of the living room—no phones in sight—she eventually located the phone in the kitchen: a shiny rectangle lying innocently on the table—lifeless. Rose looked at its black

4

screen accusingly just as it started ringing again. Georgiana's smiling face greeted her. So it *was* her calling. Rose grabbed the phone, turned it to silent, and put it back down, relieved. Georgiana's face remained lit for a few more seconds and then disappeared.

With the phone neutralized, she could go back to her peaceful sleep-in day. But as she turned to leave, a speech bubble popped up on the screen. The temptation was too strong; Rose snatched up the phone and read it.

I'm sorry, ok? Can you please pick up?

So they definitely had an argument. And it looked like it was Georgiana's fault. What could she have done? Nothing too bad, Rose was sure. Georgiana was all sweetness with Tyler. She acted nasty only when he wasn't around, during the rare times when Georgiana and Rose were alone together.

Georgiana was jealous of her. That was the only explanation. The sentiment was strong and reciprocated, too. Georgiana didn't like the idea of her boyfriend living with his attractive female best friend. As for Rose, she didn't appreciate Georgiana's intrusion into their friendship—or the intrusion of any of Tyler's girlfriends, for that matter.

And Georgiana was more annoying than most of the girls he dated. She went to Harvard Law with them, meaning she imposed not only on their free time, but on their school time as well. In class, she sat with them—Rose on one side, Georgiana on the other, and Tyler sandwiched in the middle. At lunch, she ate with them. When they were studying, she followed them to the library. And she was at the house so often that Rose wondered if she was trying to move in without Tyler noticing. Georgiana being beautiful and rich didn't help. Nor the fact that she was the daughter of one of the most powerful and recognized lawyers in Boston, Bradley Smithson.

This was the first time since high school that Tyler had dated someone who was in school with them. Rose had forgotten how hard it was to have a daily reminder of him being with someone else. Not to mention the unwelcome novelty of being in the next room when Georgiana spent the night. Contractors should make thicker walls. It was almost like Georgiana was being a loud lover on purpose, to make sure Rose knew just how well Tyler satisfied her in bed. *Her*. Not Rose. Never Rose.

When Tyler had first started going out with Georgiana, it hadn't been so hard. Not while Rose had been with her boyfriend Marcus, her longest relationship to date. She suspected the two years she'd spent with Marcus had been Tyler's first experience with jealousy. She remembered being glad when he'd started dating Georgiana so she could finally stop feeling guilty for spending all her time with her boyfriend. Rose also hadn't told Tyler she was moving in with Marcus and hadn't been sure how he would take the news. Then everything had collapsed. Marcus had been offered a huge promotion in LA. And in less than a month, he'd left Rose heartbroken, with a canceled lease and nowhere to live. Of course, Tyler had stepped in immediately and invited Rose to stay in his spare bedroom. She'd accepted, grateful to have her best friend near her 24/7. Georgiana hadn't been happy about it.

Rose sat in a chair at the kitchen table and rolled Tyler's phone in her hands, tempted to snoop. She didn't know why, but it seemed important she found out why Tyler and Georgiana had argued. But if Tyler discovered her at it, he'd flay her. He'd always been protective of his things, especially his phone, at least with his girls, and usually with a good reason. Although lately, he'd been growing increasingly private with her, too. Rose felt left out, and she couldn't help but blame Georgiana.

Georgiana, who was sorry for something she'd done. *What was it?* She contemplated the black screen, trying to make up her mind. *To spy or not to spy?*

"What are you doing?"

Tyler's voice put a sharp end to her dilemma. He was standing at the foot of the stairs, wearing only a pair of gray sweat pants.

"Oh, you're awake, good!" Rose said, faking anger to cover her embarrassment at nearly being caught in the act. "Next time if you leave your phone lying around, do me a favor and put it on silent so it doesn't wake me up."

"Rose." There was an edge to his voice. "Why were you looking into my phone?"

"I wasn't looking into your phone." She dropped the phone on the table. "This thing has been ringing nonstop for almost an hour. I couldn't sleep, and it didn't seem like you were getting up anytime soon, so I came downstairs to silence it."

"If you were just putting the phone on silent, why were you sitting on a chair with it in your hands?"

Always the lawyer.

"I was trying to decide if your cuckoo girlfriend had ruined my sleep-in," Rose said, getting up. Her chair scraped loudly on the kitchen floor. "Or if I could go back to bed."

Rose stared him down; attack was the best defense. But would he believe her?

Two

Tyler

Rose's aggressive tone was familiar. It was the one she used when she got caught doing something she shouldn't and wanted to steer the attention away from herself. She was *so* busted. Tyler didn't really care if she'd tried to hack his phone. Try as she might, his password was an alphanumeric nightmare, and he was sure not even the CIA would be able to crack it. One bad experience with an above-average tech savvy girlfriend had been enough to force Tyler to up his security.

Still, what business did Rose have nosing around his things? Usually, it was hysterical girlfriends who tried to hack him, not his best friend. He kept no secrets with Rose. Well, except maybe his constant arguments about her with Georgiana. Rose had never been BFF with any of his previous girlfriends, but with Georgiana, it had been hate at first sight. On both sides. Had Rose sensed she'd been the reason for their argument? But if she wanted to know, all she had to do was ask.

Tyler was planning a way to make her confess when she stood up, and he saw what she was wearing—or rather how much she wasn't. His eyes widened and his mouth dropped open. He was used to seeing his best friend in faded loose T-shirts three or four sizes too big for her. Not in mini shorts. Definitely not in mini shorts.

Rose must have noticed his staring because she blushed bright red. Yet, she didn't lower her gaze or rush off. *Weird.* Regular Rose was so shy and reserved. So much so that in the six months they'd been living together, she'd never shown more skin than that on her ankles. When she showered, she brought her clothes in the bathroom and came out already changed. He'd never even seen her in a towel. Even when she did the wash, she planted herself outside of the tiny laundry room like a watchdog. She said she didn't want him to see her underwear because it embarrassed her. So her standing there half-naked and bold was seriously freaking him out.

Frozen, Tyler watched her walk toward him.

"Anyway, Georgiana says she's sorry," Rose said, brushing past him as she continued toward the stairs. "And before you ask, no—I didn't spy. The message popped up on the screen."

Tyler followed her, not quite able to tear his eyes from her derrière as she climbed the stairs.

11

He was shocked into silence. Seeing her like this was like being slapped in the face. He hadn't tried to sleep with her, sober or drunk, for how long now? *Two years.* Not since she'd been with Marcus, not since her last fierce refusal of his advances. That night he'd been drunk and came on to her hard. Her "no" had been equally strong, worse than an ice shower. Sobered up by her rejection, he'd never been tempted to try again. Call it a strong reality check. To him, it had become clear she wasn't interested. So Tyler had set his mind on being her friend, *just* a friend.

His reaction to her lack of clothes was a dead giveaway that he'd been kidding himself. He collapsed onto the living room couch, taking a few minutes to steady himself and reboot his brain. He'd always thought Rose was beautiful, but he'd never considered her sexy. Yet today, her outfit combined with her defiant attitude made her irresistible. He needed to know what was going on to make her act so strangely. As if pulled by an invisible rope, Tyler got to his feet and followed Rose up the stairs.

His phone remained forgotten and lonely on the kitchen table, Georgiana's face surfacing on the screen yet again.

***

At the top of the stairs, Tyler looked toward Rose's room. She'd left the door half-open. Was it an invitation?

He approached, padding quietly across the carpet, and peeked inside. Rose was lying on the bed, propped on a mound of pillows with her legs stretched out and crossed at the ankles. She was playing with her phone. To his delight, she hadn't changed, or put on a sweater. His Rose, after being caught in mini shorts, would be covered head-to-toe by now. Something was definitely up with her.

Tyler knocked on the door and stepped inside without waiting for permission.

"Oh," she said, surprised. "I thought you'd be downstairs making peace with Georgiana."

"What's up with the shorts?" he asked.

She looked down at herself. "I was behind with my laundry, and this was the only clean set left."

"Weren't you against Victoria's Secret and their objectification of women?" Tyler retorted.

"I didn't buy them." Rose shrugged. "They were a present from Marcus."

She said it casually, but he knew her well. He could detect the lingering sadness hidden behind that simple response. As a loyal friend, he ought to feel sorry for the abrupt way her relationship with Marcus had ended. Instead, Tyler couldn't help but be relieved that Marcus had moved to LA and out of their lives for good. But now a new emotion had entered the mix—a fierce jealousy he'd never experienced before. He was jealous that Rose would wear something so not like herself for Marcus.

Tyler sat on the bed next to her. He took her right foot into his left hand, placed it in his lap, and started massaging her ankle. *Time to switch on the charm and make Rose talk.*

Three

Rose

Rose was extremely aware of Tyler's thumb swirling around her ankle. How long had it been since he'd tried to sleep with her? Tyler had been "well-behaved" since that stupid night two years ago when she'd refused him in no uncertain terms. She almost flinched at the memory. At the time, she'd been so taken with Marcus that she'd been harsh with her best friend, treating him with contempt—and not in their usual playful way. Rose hoped Tyler had been drunk enough not to remember how badly she'd turned him down. But given that he hadn't tried anything ever since, not even after her breakup, some of it must've sunk in. Before that night, his cute, double-meaning jokes and her constant turning him down had let Rose believe she and Tyler weren't together by her choice. That if she only wanted, she could be his girlfriend. That he'd be different for her. But not anymore.

A tingle rose up her legs from where Tyler touched her with the tips of his fingers. It had been easier to say no to Tyler when he was hitting on her once a week. But now she was out of practice and vulnerable. Especially when he was standing in her room looking impossibly hot in sweatpants and nothing else. Rose's gaze traveled over his naked chest and down to his sculpted stomach before she forced herself to adopt a neck-and-above only view policy. Not that staring at his face helped. With messy light brown hair, gray eyes, and lips to die for, Tyler was gorgeous. And he knew it.

"So what's up with Georgiana?" Rose put her phone down and looked at Tyler expectantly.

"Oh, nothing," he replied.

"It must've been something if she felt the need to call you ten times on a Saturday morning."

"I've already told you it was nothing."

"So why was she sorry about nothing?"

"Why do you have to always insist so much when it comes to Georgiana?"

"And why are you so adamant about not telling me? You used to tell me everything!"

"I still do."

"No, you don't."

Tyler's shoulder tensed and his grip on her feet tightened. "I can't stand the two of you bickering anymore. I'm always caught in the middle."

"I've never said anything bad about Georgiana," Rose said, feeling her cheeks warm up. "But apparently she doesn't have a problem talking behind my back."

Tyler held her gaze for a few seconds before looking at the floor, embarrassed.

Comprehension dawned. "The argument, it *was* about me, wasn't it?" Rose said, leaning forward. She folded her legs, her ankle slipping away from Tyler's grip. "Why does she hate me so much?"

"Don't be melodramatic. She's just jealous, that's all."

"Why am I the only friend she's jealous about? Especially when I'm the only one you haven't slept with."

"Well, you're the only friend who lives with me. And Georgiana has this theory: the fact we haven't slept together is more meaningful than if we had. She actually said she wished we'd done it before I met her and got over it!"

"And what exactly makes Georgiana think sleeping with me would make you get over us?"

"Would it?" Tyler asked with a hint of flirtation. He raised one eyebrow and smirked, making one of his cutest, mischievous faces.

"It doesn't matter. We're not going to test it." Rose kept her sulky frown. "So, what was she going on about this time?"

Tyler released a breath. "Georgiana asked me when you were planning on moving out."

Rose shot out of the bed as if it were made of burning coals. "I didn't know I'd overstayed my welcome," she spat. It was just like Georgiana to stick her posh nose into Rose's life, where it didn't belong.

True, Rose was living in Tyler's swanky apartment without paying any rent. But only because Tyler didn't let her pay her share. To compensate, Rose did what she could. She bought most of the groceries and paid all the bills. Even though she and Tyler had never spoken about it, she thought he was fine with their arrangement. Georgiana had already made a snarky comment once to her: "How nice it must be to live rent-free in such a nice neighborhood." Rose could only imagine what other things along that line she was telling Tyler. The thought made her livid.

"I can start packing immediately." Rose moved to grab some discarded clothes from a chair.

"Rose, will you calm down?" Tyler said, grabbing her wrist and pulling her onto his lap. "I've told Georgiana to piss off."

"You know I feel guilty about not paying rent," she protested, trying to ignore the fact that she was sitting on top of him and they were both half-naked.

"And you know I don't want you to pay anything. You already sneak around and pay all the bills before I even have a chance to open them. It's more than enough."

He put his hands around her waist, making her stomach drop.

"Are you sure?" Rose asked. She needed more than just a physical assurance.

"Rose, my life has improved since you moved in with me. The fridge used to look like a war zone, but now you make sure I eat all my vegetables," he joked.

"I bet she just wants me out so *she* can move in," Rose couldn't help saying.

"As if." Tyler snorted, and the goofy sound made Rose happier than she'd been all morning.

She beamed at him, looking him straight in the eyes. Tyler stared back with a strange intensity, and suddenly, Rose's smile disappeared. He leaned in closer, slowly, and her breath caught in her throat in anticipation.

Four

Georgiana

A few miles away, in another posh neighborhood of Boston, Georgiana paced around her living room. As she circled the couch, she was seething with hatred for Rose, anger for Tyler, and resentment for Marcus. Whom she didn't exactly know, but who she was positively sure had ruined her life by moving to LA.

She tried Tyler's number again. When he didn't pick up, she threw her phone across the room and let out a growl. The phone hit an armchair and bounced off its soft cushions, landing on the carpeted floor.

This wasn't going to work. Another woman living with Tyler wasn't right. How could he not see it? What was his house, a stupid co-ed? A charity? Georgiana didn't know for sure, but since Rose and Tyler came from the same rich neighborhood in Dallas, she doubted Rose had money problems. She was just a parasite. Tyler's best friend was poison ivy, and she was sprouting roots in his house.

Why wasn't he picking up his damn phone?

Georgiana checked the time on her Rolex: 9:45 already. She'd been calling him for almost an hour now. Bracing her arms on the back of the couch, Georgiana stared out of her floor-to-ceiling windows without focusing on anything in particular. Maybe his phone was switched to silent and he hadn't heard it ring. What if Tyler was still asleep? It wasn't unusual for him to sleep late on weekends, and they'd been arguing until the small hours last night. Tyler had left her apartment at— three, four a.m.? By the time he'd gotten home and to bed, it must've been late.

That was it, she decided, Tyler was still sleeping. Nothing to worry about. Yeah, they had a row, and he'd taken Rose's side, *again,* but it would pass. It always did.

Georgiana's nervous fingers tightened their grip on the soft cushions fabric. *Men*! They could sleep through everything. Unlike her. She'd barely slept and had been forced to use all of her willpower not to call him before nine—Georgiana didn't want to come off as the hysterical girlfriend.

Anyway, Tyler asleep or not, the problem remained. Georgiana needed to weed the poisonous bitch out of her boyfriend's place. The sneaky little ho was after her man. She'd probably been since puberty. Why did Marcus have to dump Rose and give her the perfect excuse to move in with Tyler? To feed off his generosity and good nature?

If Tyler and Rose stayed under the same roof much longer, something was bound to happen. Tyler's relationship with Rose wasn't strictly brotherly—no matter how many times Tyler swore it was. Georgiana didn't believe in male-female friendships. And their body language sent a clear message: there was tension between them. The fact they hadn't done the deed yet wasn't an assurance it would not happen in the future. It was even worse, in a way. It built pressure, making Rose—the one girl Tyler had never had—too big of a temptation for him to resist.

Why did everything have to go down this way? And why now?

Georgiana felt as if a cosmic conspiracy was in place to undermine her relationship with Tyler. But she wasn't a "live and let live" kind of girl. She was used to taking action and gaining control over things. She'd even tried to convince her brother to provide a distraction for Rose as soon as she'd moved in with Tyler six months ago. Ethan, five years their senior, was drop dead gorgeous and a womanizer. But he'd refused without even meeting Rose. And now was dating one of Georgiana's best friends, Alice, so his charms were out of the picture. To hell with him, too. Georgiana needed a different plan, something final that would keep Tyler and Rose apart for good.

Georgiana turned away from the window and started pacing the apartment again in search of inspiration. It took her a few laps of the room before an idea began forming in her mind. At first, she couldn't quite grasp it. Georgiana was sure she'd overlooked something, but couldn't put her finger on what. Then, out of the blue, a possibility came to her. She needed to talk to her dad and see if he could help her.

Georgiana sprang into action. She grabbed her bag and car keys from the coffee table and hurried toward the door. Halfway there, she paused and turned around to go get her phone. She picked it up from the floor and checked the screen, only half-hoping to see if Tyler had called her back. He hadn't.

Never mind, he could wait. Right now, she had bigger fish to fry. Filled with purpose, Georgiana plonked the phone into her bag and exited her apartment. She felt strangely calm and regenerated. It was good to finally have a plan.

It'd be complicated to achieve, and she'd have to pull a lot of strings to make it work. Hard, but not impossible. And, *oh*, Rose wouldn't even know what had hit her. Georgiana opened her car and sat behind the wheel. She paused a second with her finger on the ignition button. She closed her eyes, imagining the face her rival would make when she found out. It'd be priceless. But now wasn't the time to celebrate, it was the time to set her plan in motion. To pull it off, she had to act quickly. Georgiana revved the engine and backed out of her parking spot, speeding away on the almost empty street.

Five

Tyler

Tyler watched the smile disappear from Rose's face, dazed by her beauty. Her dark eyes sent a clear message. It wasn't his best friend staring at him, but a woman who wanted him. After all this time, would she finally give in? Today, of all days, when he'd least expect it, and when he hadn't tried one of his many stunts to seduce her?

His pulse picked up, and his skin started to burn around his neck where Rose laced her hands. Suddenly, Tyler realized where they were. In her room, on the bed, already half-naked and on top of each other.

Rose's face was only inches away from his own—one breath away. Tyler leaned in closer as if to kiss her and felt her body stiffen on his legs, but she didn't move away. Nor did she make any motion to get up. Rose's eyes widened, and she inhaled sharply, but she didn't retreat.

Tyler didn't need any more hints. This was his opportunity; he would not waste this chance and give Rose time to think about what was happening or to change her mind. He bent her backward and pressed his lips to hers.

***

Afterward, Tyler lay in Rose's bed. He was staring at the ceiling mesmerized by what had just happened, and cherishing the weight of her body on his chest as she slept. Tyler trailed a finger down her neck, to her shoulder, and down her arm. Rose shivered without waking up, and then her breathing relaxed again.

Tyler was stunned by what had just happened between them. Finally, he understood what making love meant as opposed to having sex. Everything happened spontaneously with no inhibitions. Even if it was their first time together, they knew each other too well to be shy. At least in the passion of the moment. And making love to Rose had been unique, explosive, and urgent, like taking that first breath of air after being underwater for a long time. Why had they waited so long? The last ten years seemed like a total waste of time now. But that was over. Everything would change now.

Guilt tightened his chest, the same sensation that ripped through Tyler whenever he cheated on any of his girlfriends. With Georgiana, he'd honestly thought things would be different. His girlfriend was cool, never too clingy, and—except for the subject of Rose staying with him—they never argued about anything. And now Tyler could see Georgiana had been right all along. She'd picked up on something he'd been blind to.

He'd have to break up with her at once. Tyler wasn't looking forward to that "friendly" chat. He was sure Georgiana would not make it easy for him. But there was no space left in his life for her, not now that his friendship with Rose had transformed into something new, something better...

Could it be possible he'd been in love with his best friend all these years without ever realizing it? Was this why he'd cheated in all his previous relationships? Because he'd never loved any of the girls he'd dated?

Tyler had always been attracted to Rose. But he'd always assumed it was a natural I-am-a-boy-you-are-a-girl kind of attraction. Nothing more. Today, he was no longer sure about anything. All the air had left his lungs and his heart wouldn't stop racing. Whenever he had a flashback of the past hour, his stomach contracted as if plunging down a steep rollercoaster ride. Was this what being in love felt like?

The L-word sent a thrill of fear down his spine. This was Rose in his arms; he couldn't screw this one up. He had to be cautious and take it slow, one day at a time. He looked down at her. Rose was snuggled against him, her head resting on his chest, her eyes closed. He brushed the hair away from her face to have a clear view of her beautiful, serene features as she slept.

Yep, he was in trouble.

Six

Rose

Rose kept her eyes tightly shut, pretending she was still asleep, despite Tyler trailing a finger down her arm. She was sure the loud thuds of her heart would soon give her away, but she didn't know what to do next. After what just happened between them, was her friendship with Tyler ruined forever?

Rose was mad at herself for being so weak. Today, she hadn't been able to resist. Not with Georgiana being a bitch. Not with Marcus dumping her and leaving her as insecure as ever. And not with Tyler being Tyler.

Oh, Tyler! He was a lost cause. A romantic relationship between them was impossible. Hope for a future with Tyler had died a long time ago. Rose spent years waiting for him to change, not dating anyone, sticking around for when he'd be mature enough or for the girl of the moment to be dumped. Until she'd finally accepted he would never change.

Unbidden, her mind began a mental recap of all the girls Tyler had dated over the years. He had sex for the first time during sophomore year in high school with Amanda Lockwood, a junior. Amanda was a popular girl, and after his conquest, Tyler became the hero of the school. Despite girls finding him irresistible, he remained faithful to Amanda for a whole year; after all, she was his first. They were happy together until summer break when Amanda's nemesis, Charlotte Pierce, seduced him during summer break. With Amanda gone for a month, teenage Tyler was easy prey for Charlotte.

When Amanda found out, drama ensued. Amanda and Charlotte became the first entries on a long list of girls who would end up hating Tyler for cheating on and dumping them. By twelfth grade, Tyler was the most popular guy in school, basking in the glory of fooling around with a never-ending stream of girls.

Rose had hoped college would steady him. Instead, it sent him on an even wilder spree. In their freshman year at Harvard, Tyler slept with a different girl almost every night. Rose told herself it was only their first year; once he got it out of his system, he would be ready for something serious. Across their sophomore and junior year, hope returned briefly as Tyler stayed in a serious relationship with Jessica, an English major he'd met at the library. Tyler and Jessica were together for nine months before Tyler cheated on her, making Rose officially give up on him. If he couldn't stay true to Jessica, the closest thing he'd ever had to a long-term girlfriend, then how could Rose trust him with her own heart?

After Jessica, it had been the same story with every new girlfriend. He cheated on all of them, and they each ended up loathing him. Rose didn't want to end up loathing her best friend; he was the most important person in her life besides her parents. He was family. And she knew a romantic relationship would lead exactly to that. In the end, he'd cheat on her—if not in a year, in five, or ten. It was a given. Tyler simply wasn't a monogamist. Rose would end up bitter, with her heart shattered. Today had been a mistake, a big one. But they could fix it. They had to.

Rose stirred as if just now waking up. She looked at Tyler shyly, blushing.

"What?" she asked, self-consciously pulling the sheets around her body.

Tyler flashed her a mischievous grin. "I find it funny you choose to blush now."

"I didn't choose to, and don't look at me like that."

"Like what?"

His wolfish smile was making it impossible to keep a steady mind.

"As if you want to eat me."

"Maybe I do." Tyler bit her hand affectionately.

"Pff." Rose's face burned red, so she buried it in his chest to cover up her uneasiness. Shame attacked as she replayed the past hour in her head in an all-consuming vortex of emotions. *Oh*, the things Tyler had done to her, and the way she'd responded! It wasn't just sex—Tyler had made love to her. Or had it all been a dream?

Unable to meet his gaze yet, Rose burrowed her face deeper.

"Don't play shy, Rosalynn," Tyler said, using her full name. He planted a soft kiss on her collarbone. *No, definitely not a dream.* "After today, I won't buy it."

After today. That's the problem.

She shifted position so that he couldn't kiss her. "So…" she began.

"I know that expression, Rosalynn Atwood. It's your serious-talk one."

"Tyler. This is serious."

"What's serious?"

"Me, you, naked in bed."

"Relax, Rose. It's not the end of the world."

"No, but it could be the end of our friendship. Doesn't that scare you?"

"What do you mean?" he asked, frowning.

Tears welled in Rose's eyes. Emotions were running high, and her throat closed, making it difficult to get the words out. "I think it was a mistake."

"Why?"

"All your exes hate you."

"What's that supposed to mean?"

"You cheated on all of them."

"That's not true."

"Name one you haven't."

Tyler scrunched his face for a while and then said, "I haven't cheated on Georgiana."

"Oh, right, your girlfriend!" Hearing him say her name sent Rose into a frenzy. "The one you *just cheated on*!"

"But it was with you, so it doesn't count."

"I don't think Georgiana would agree."

Tyler shrugged, unconcerned. "I can dump her if that's what's bothering you."

"How nice of you," she replied with an edge. "Please, don't dump her on my account."

"Rose, I wouldn't cheat on you."

"How do you know?" She narrowed her eyes at him. "Do you really expect me to trust you'd be fine sleeping with me, and only with me, for the rest of your life?"

"Yes. No. What the hell do I know! I haven't even had breakfast and you're already talking marriage. Why don't we choose the name of our kids already and be done with it?"

"It's not like we can date and see how it goes, right?" Rose bit back.

"Why not? What's wrong with that?"

"Everything's wrong with that."

"Nothing's wrong with that."

"Tyler, please stop talking. You're making it worse."

"I don't get you, Rose. What do you want me to say?"

"Nothing. You've already said enough."

"Why do you girls have to go cuckoo the moment the sex is over?"

"See, Tyler, that's the problem. I'm not one of your girls, and I'll never be." Rose sat up, leaning away from him. "This was a big mistake. I wasn't thinking."

"I preferred you when you weren't."

"Well, I am now. This," she added, flipping a finger between them, "shouldn't have happened. It won't happen again." Rose gathered the bed linens around her, transforming into a human cocoon to shield her naked body from him, and further retreated to her side of the bed.

"Don't worry, Rose," Tyler said, grabbing his pants and pulling them on. "I'll get out of your way."

He jumped off the bed and was out of the room in three quick strides. He slammed the door behind him, making her chest jolt. The knot in her throat worsened.

The moment Tyler left, Rose felt dead inside. She reached out her hand to his side of the bed where the sheets were still warm from his body heat. Tears pricked her eyes again. She wasn't ready to let him go, not yet.

Still wrapped in the sheets, Rose followed him out of the room. In the hall, she paused to listen. The shower was running. Rose tried the bathroom door. *Unlocked.* Turning the knob, she pushed the door open and tiptoed into the room. As expected, Tyler was in the shower. She tapped on the glass, the sound barely audible over the water noise.

He flung the glass door open and stared at her in shock. With a pounding heart, Rose let the bed sheet drop to the floor and stepped into the shower with him. Tyler raised his eyebrows. He probably thought she was crazy. She'd just said sleeping together had been a mistake. Yet, here she was, jumping him in the shower not two minutes later.

"Today doesn't count," Rose said curtly, answering his unspoken question. She stood on tiptoes and pulled him toward her in a wet kiss.

Seven

Rose

The next day ended up not counting as well. And the next. And the next.

Rose and Tyler fell into a weird routine of having sex (making love?) wherever, whenever, without ever talking about it. Afterward, they pretended nothing had happened. Rose knew she was playing a dangerous game, one impossible to win. She knew Tyler wasn't ready for a serious relationship with her, but she couldn't help herself. Even if having an affair with Tyler was so wrong, for so many reasons.

For one, it put their friendship, the most important thing in her life, at stake. Then there was the obvious moral issue: Tyler still had a girlfriend. He hadn't broken up with Georgiana. And even if he didn't bring her to the house anymore, he was still with her. Was he sleeping with her too? On the odd nights when he didn't come home and stayed at her place, Rose cried herself to sleep in her room. For the next few days, she would pout and ignore Tyler, but eventually, she'd break. Then she would jump right back into his arms, and their unhealthy routine started all over.

Another week like this—another day—and she'd go crazy. The right thing to do would be to stop. But Rose didn't know how to be strong, not anymore. She'd wanted Tyler for too long to be able to keep saying no. Rose told herself she preferred to be the one he was cheating *with*, instead of the one he was cheating *on*. After a month, however, even this excuse was running thin.

True, Rose had told him he didn't have to leave Georgiana for her, but that had been ages ago! After a month of sleeping together, everything was different. How could Tyler not see it? She refused to beg him—what if he said no? What if he said *yes*? They'd get together, and then he'd cheat on her. Nothing terrified Rose more. On one hand, she wanted Tyler to leave Georgiana and be with her officially. On the other, it scared her to death. Unsure of everything else, the only thing Rose knew for a fact was that her life couldn't keep going like this.

Something had to change, soon, but Rose didn't know what, or how.

Tyler

For the first time in his life, Tyler didn't understand his best friend. How to read her, how to translate what she said as opposed to what went on inside her head. Rose had been adamant they shouldn't be together. Not unless he proposed right then and there, and he wasn't ready for that kind of commitment. At twenty-four and still in school, who the hell would be? He didn't want to be tied down already. But Rose had become a drug for him. He couldn't go back to being just her friend, and he couldn't be with her, either—not in the way she wanted.

Screwed, he was so screwed.

Georgiana was driving him mad, too. His girlfriend wasn't stupid, and she must have sensed his emotional distance. The few nights she forced him to stay at her apartment, he pretended to be tired to avoid sleeping with her, and he never invited her to the house anymore. They were arguing more often than not, and he was getting tired. And school hadn't even started yet. His love life was proving more stressful than Harvard Law. To survive one was hard, but the two combined? *Impossible.* How would he handle the pressure in less than a month when the academic year started?

What would happen when he'd have to spend all his days in class squeezed between the two women in his life? It would be a disaster, no doubt. He should dump Georgiana, but the idea scared him. If he became single, what would happen with Rose? Wedding bells? And what would happen if he kept a girlfriend on the side to avoid commitment?

If he didn't do something, the situation with Rose and Georgiana was going to explode in his face. But what could he do? Tyler was stuck, strangled in a situation of his own making, with no escape in sight. He wished girls came with an instruction manual. The only thing he knew was that his life couldn't keep going like this.

Something had to change, soon, but Tyler didn't know what, or how.

Georgiana

Something was up with Tyler. No sex since the night of their fight about Rose moving out of his apartment. That was a month ago. *A month.* Whenever Georgiana tried initiating, Tyler mumbled some lame excuse about being tired. Usually, he couldn't keep his hands off her, and now nothing for a month. *Thirty. Freaking. Days.* He also made it clear she wasn't welcome at his apartment anymore. Why? What did he have to hide?

If not with her, he was sleeping with someone else. Rose? It must be that bitch. Why keep his girlfriend away from the house otherwise?

Georgiana was almost certain something had happened between them. When she finally admitted to herself that her boyfriend was cheating on her, Georgiana went to a dark place. She shut herself in her apartment without eating and without getting out of bed for two days. Tyler didn't check on her once. His conspicuous absence and indifference transformed the numbing pain in a rampaging fury. The blind rage manifested in a strong desire to burn Tyler's expensive car to the ground. She'd also been tempted to dump him without ever looking back. But then her pride took over. She discovered she didn't care if he'd cheated on her—she was in love with Tyler. He was hers, and she was ready to fight for him. She wasn't going to let that ho snatch him away from her. No matter what it took, Georgiana was determined to keep Tyler. But their relationship couldn't keep going like this.

Something had to change, soon, and Georgiana knew exactly what, and how.

Eight

Rose

"Rose, can you please pass me the ketchup bottle?" Georgiana asked, her tone so viciously polite, she might as well have said, "I know what you did."

Rose lowered her gaze. Georgiana's razor sharp blue eyes were too much for her now. "Sure." She took the red plastic bottle and handed it to Tyler's girlfriend.

Two weeks later, and not only had her "situation" with Tyler not resolved—or improved, or changed at all—now she was also having lunch with the happy couple in a cafeteria on campus. The fall semester hadn't started yet, but it was orientation period, and the campus was already buzzing with students. How in hell did this lunch happen? The three of them eating burgers together was too weird.

Tyler's text, "lunch 2gether," had been innocent enough; it didn't say, "Georgiana the Ice Queen will attend too," anywhere, not even a hint. Since their affair, Tyler had avoided any unnecessary contact between *mistress* and

41

girlfriend. Rose suspected Georgiana must've orchestrated the lunch trapping them here.

But, why? Did she know? That had to be it. Georgiana knew about her and Tyler, and now she would slowly torture them until they confessed. No matter how many fake smiles Georgiana shot Rose, they never reached her cold, calculating eyes. That freezing blue gaze sent Rose a clear message, "I hate you."

Rose studied Georgiana as she sat possessively next to Tyler, eating all his fries. Did she know Rose loved eating his fries? Was her dominion over his French fries a metaphor for their love triangle? Rose hated that out in the open Tyler belonged to Georgiana, and that she, *the other woman*, was powerless about it.

"Rose," Georgiana said, still all sweetness, "do you have any plans for this coming Friday?"

"No, nothing in particular," Rose said cautiously.

This had to be an ambush or some kind of plot—Georgiana never asked about her "plans." Not to mention she was still being uncharacteristically nice. Had Tyler's girlfriend decided to kill her with kindness? Rose wasn't a fan of this sudden change; it was easier to sneak around with Tyler behind her back when Georgiana was being a bitch to her. If she considered Georgiana a nice, normal girl, then Rose's guilt would overwhelm her. The Ice Queen almost certainly had an ulterior motive.

"Oh, that's perfect!" Georgiana exclaimed. "I'm having a dinner with some friends for my birthday. I want you to be there. Will you come?"

Rose couldn't think of a polite way to say no. "Um... yeah, sure. Where?"

"Great." Georgiana's lips parted in a cruel grin. "I haven't decided yet. But you can come with Tyler straight from your house. I'll meet you there."

"Okay."

Even more peculiar. Georgiana not bugging Tyler to pick her up and instead suggesting he chauffeured Rose. Something was definitely up.

Tyler

Tyler followed the exchange, at a loss for words. He pushed his plate away, his stomach churning. What was Georgiana planning? She'd already thrown him a curve ball impossible to catch. He was trapped; what else did she need?

He should've left her when he had the chance. He should've known Georgiana wouldn't stand idly by while he was having his way with Rose. That his conniving girlfriend would fight. And she had. She'd fought and won, at least the first battle: make sure Tyler and Rose didn't share a roof. Heck, make sure they didn't live in the same continent!

Tyler smiled a bitter smile. He had to give it to Georgiana. She was resourceful. Even without proof, he was sure she had orchestrated everything. Scholarships abroad did not reopen out of the blue. Georgiana's doing or not, the damage was done, and Tyler was left with no other choice other than when to tell Rose. No turning back time at this point.

He looked at his best friend with longing. He'd have to talk to her soon, but Tyler couldn't bear the thought of losing her. And after talking to her, he'd consider himself lucky if she ever spoke two words to him again.

***

Friday night, on the way to the restaurant, Tyler still hadn't spoken to Rose. He'd vowed to do it tonight after they got back home, but maybe it had been a mistake to wait a week. It'd only make Rose angrier. And the prospect of Rose and Georgiana in the same room for a whole dinner made him nervous. An ominous feeling about the party crept up his back and settled heavily on his shoulders.

Rose sat in silence beside him, staring out the window. She was holding a tiny gift-wrapped package in her hands. He'd told her it wasn't necessary to buy Georgiana a present, but Rose had insisted. Thinking about it, he had no clue what was in the box. Something poisonous? Tyler could only hope.

At home, Rose had stunned him again. She'd emerged from her room dressed in a tight black jumpsuit with cutouts around the waist, and an almost bare back. She was also wearing black heels and a furry-leathery jacket thingy. The outfit looked like a Catwoman costume. Rose was only missing the ears, whiskers, and tail. Again, he'd never seen these clothes before. He was discovering an entirely new side of her she'd kept secret all this time. And even if it was great to see Rose in a different light, sometimes Tyler wished he were still oblivious. His life would be much simpler without the temptation.

This sort of gear must've been reserved for Marcus. Jealousy made Tyler swallow hard. He still hated Rose's ex with all his guts, but tonight the sexiness was for him, or to compete with

Georgiana. To be honest, he didn't know which one.

Tyler's skittish mood worsened as they entered the restaurant. Georgiana and some of her guests were already there, sitting at a long, rectangular table laid for at least twenty people. Georgiana sat at the head of the table with an empty space on her left, followed by a couple of nicely dressed girls. On her right sat a rather plain guy followed by two other girls and another arrogant-looking dude who seemed older than everyone else. Fifteen or so empty places were left at the table.

The older guy fixated his gaze on Rose the moment she entered the door. Noticing the competition, Tyler felt an immediate, irrational surge of hatred for the stranger. For no other reason than the way he was looking at Rose, Tyler wanted to punch the dude's face.

Nine

Rose

Walking inside the restaurant, Rose watched Georgiana rise to her feet to greet them. Tyler's girlfriend looked resplendent in a short dress made of lace flowers, white from the waist up and pale pink on the skirt.

"You've made it!" she said. "Here, come meet the others." She did a quick round of introduction, starting counterclockwise and working around the whole table.

Rose stood there awkwardly, looking around at half a dozen strangers. In particular, the guy sitting at the edge of the group, who Georgiana introduced as Ethan, made her self-conscious with all his staring. Rose met his gaze shyly. He had bright, unsettling light blue eyes that looked somewhat familiar. Short black hair, high cheekbones, and a square jaw made the dude good-looking in that arrogant vampire-flick-villain kind of way.

Embarrassed by all the attention, Rose delivered her gift to Georgiana—a noncommittal makeup palette—who thanked her without opening the present. With nothing left to do, Rose wanted to shrink away and play invisible for the rest of the evening. Sitting down was the first camouflaging step. A quick scan of the table told Rose where she stood in the food chain. The seat beside Her Birthday Majesty was obviously intended for Tyler, and the ones nearest for her court. Rose didn't want to be anywhere near the couple, anyway, so she backtracked to the opposite end of the table. Georgiana protested with no real conviction that she shouldn't sit so far away, but Rose assured her majesty she'd be fine, and Georgiana didn't insist further.

Rose had a hunch about the night ending badly for her. She'd never seen Georgiana look so radiant, so smug. At this very moment, Georgiana was watching Rose with an expression in-between triumph and pity. Why? Something was happening, and Rose felt like the only clueless party present. Tyler had been behaving strangely all week, and she couldn't tell what had changed. Combining that with the evil stare above Georgiana's smiles only increased her anxiety about this party. What on earth had made her agree to come?

The moment Rose sat down, Ethan got up and whispered something in Georgiana's ear. He took his half-empty cocktail with him and moved toward Rose. The dude was tall, although maybe an inch or two shorter than Tyler. Speaking of the devil, she stole a glance at Tyler for just a second. He wore an expression of contempt on his face as he followed Ethan's movements. *Good. Serves him right to be the jealous one for a change.*

Rose looked around at the other guests and spotted another hostile gaze, only this one was targeting *her*. The blonde girl who'd been sitting next to Ethan didn't appear at all happy with his move. *Don't glare at me, lady. I didn't ask your guy to come talk to me. Is he even your guy?*

"Hello," Ethan said as he took the seat next to her. "It didn't seem right to have you sit here all alone. I'm Ethan, Georgiana's brother."

Ah, that explains why the eyes looked familiar.

"And you're Rose, right?" he continued.

"Right." She smiled at him, blushing under his piercing gaze despite herself. Was this what Tyler felt whenever Georgiana looked at him? Rose's heart sank into her chest.

Ethan

Ethan was intrigued by the faint blush that appeared on Rose's cheeks as he spoke to her. In fact, he was intrigued by everything about Rose. When his sister had begged him to seduce her boyfriend's new roommate, she'd described Rose as austere-looking, but pretty. The woman seated next to him was neither austere nor pretty. To call Rose pretty would be the understatement of the millennium. She was a dark beauty with her long brown hair, olive skin, and almost-black eyes. And to think he'd wanted to stay at the office tonight.

"So, how do you know my sister?" he asked, feigning cluelessness.

"We're at Harvard Law together, and she's dating my best friend Tyler," Rose said.

"You came here together?"

"Yeah, I'm crashing at his place until I can find one of my own. I had a lease mishap."

"What kind of mishap?" Ethan asked. Georgiana had already filled him in on the drama with the ex-boyfriend, but he wanted to see if Rose would volunteer the information.

She did. "Oh, nothing serious. My ex-boyfriend dumped me a month before we were supposed to move in together, and I'd already canceled my lease on my old place." Rose shrugged, smiling awkwardly.

Ethan realized he liked her even more after her straightforward answer.

"So, being Georgiana's brother, can I safely assume you're a lawyer?" Rose asked.

"I am afraid you can't," he said with a naughty smile.

"You didn't go to Harvard Law? I thought every offspring of the Smithson family went to Harvard."

"I did go to Harvard Law, as did all my siblings and cousins before and after me," Ethan replied, amused by the way she'd wrinkled her nose in confusion.

"And after all that pain, you didn't become a lawyer?"

"Actually, I did."

"I don't understand," Rose said. "What happened?"

"I tried the big studio with the big cases and the long hours for a year and hated it, so I quit."

"And your father let you?"

"He had little a choice. I'm over eighteen, you know."

"You stood up to Bradley Smithson. I'm impressed."

Ethan roared with laughter. "To me, he's just Dad."

"So he didn't make a fuss?" she asked.

"Of course he did. But in the end, when he saw my mind was set, all he could do was make me pay him back my tuitions."

"For law school?"

"And college, too."

"Ouch." Rose winced. "And you managed?"

"Just about. I'm still paying. Having him as a creditor makes me regret not taking out student loans."

"So what do you do now?"

"I'm in real estate." Ethan scrutinized her face for a reaction. Was she going to give him the downright sorrowful look of contempt other lawyers reserved for him when he told them his new occupation?

She didn't.

"My father is in real estate," Rose said. "What do you do, exactly?"

"I buy places that need refurbishing and restore them. When I'm done, I re-sell them or rent them out."

"If you have some nice studio apartments to rent, you could show them to me," she said and then looked away as if she immediately regretted her words.

"So you're looking to move out?" Ethan said, his eyes never leaving her face.

He saw her throw a furtive, guilty glance at Tyler, who was looking back at her pointedly. "I mean, not that I have much of a budget," she backtracked.

"I'll see what I can do," he promised. "If something interesting pops up, you'll be the first one I call."

Ethan meant the words. For once, he found himself united with his sister and her wishing for Tyler and Rose not to live under the same roof. From what he'd gathered from Georgiana on their way here, he didn't think it'd be a problem for much longer. Still, Ethan wanted Rose out of Tyler's house as soon as possible. Why? He wasn't sure yet. He just recognized it as a fact.

Ten

Rose

Once all the guests had arrived, menus were distributed and Rose picked one up as an excuse to conclude the conversation with Ethan.

She stared at the pages, not really reading them. Instead, she felt guilty for lying about her need for an apartment, or for it to be on a budget. Well, not exactly lied. Her dad was in real estate; she'd just omitted that his company owned half of Dallas, where she and Tyler were from. Rose wasn't as comfortable as Tyler when it came to displaying her family's wealth. Yes, she asked her dad to help with money. But only to cover her tuition and limited living expenses. So it was sort of true she was on a budget for her rent, even if the budget was self-imposed.

What wasn't true was that she was looking for a house. She had no intention of moving out of Tyler's home.

Rose focused on the menu, for real this time, but didn't understand what she was supposed to order. What were a nigiri, a maki, or a miso? There were no pictures to provide context, as the restaurant was definitely too classy for those. Yeah, everyone was supposed to eat sushi and speak foodie-Japanese these days, and it was unsophisticated of her not to, but she couldn't digest the idea of eating raw fish. The concept made her slightly nauseous.

"Pssst," she whispered with her face hidden behind the leather menu.

"Are you talking to me?" Ethan asked, cocking his head toward her.

"Mm-hmm. Are you a sushi connoisseur?"

"I've had my fair share. Why?" He spoke with his whole head hidden behind the black menu and his face turned toward hers.

"I don't have the faintest idea what any of this is. Can you help me out?"

"You've never had sushi?" Ethan seemed shocked.

"I'm from Texas where eating something that hasn't been barbequed, or at least grilled, is considered a state offense."

"You're from Texas! But you don't have a southern accent."

"My mom is from Chicago. But we moved here ages ago for college."

"Your mom and you?" Ethan asked.

"Oh. No, I meant Tyler and me." Rose shifted uncomfortably in her seat, not sure she wanted to talk about Tyler with Ethan. "We've known each other since preschool. He's like family."

"Family, huh?" Ethan appeared skeptical. Was she such an open book?

She deliberately changed the subject. "Will you order for me?"

He laughed. "Sure."

"I want something like a beginner set of the less gross things."

"By 'gross,' I'll assume you're referring to the raw fish. In case you didn't know, they also have cooked stuff here—you want me to get you one of those?"

"You know what? I don't think I'll give sushi another try any time soon, so I might as well go all in with the uncooked bits."

"Mmm, you're the adventurous type." Ethan winked one of those daring blue eyes at her, causing her stomach to do a little involuntary flip. "I like it."

When their food arrived, Rose found herself in another predicament—she did not grasp the use of chopsticks.

"Ethan?" she murmured. It was the first time she said his name, and she liked the sound of it.

"How can I be of assistance?"

"Do you think they'd flay me if I asked for a fork and a knife?"

He chuckled. "You're helpless, aren't you?"

"I'd like to see you fight a full rack of greasy barbequed pork ribs with your bare hands in your neat white shirt," she joked. "Then it'd be my turn to laugh."

Ethan chuckled again. "Japanese actually eat sushi with their hands. It's supposed to be eaten that way, at least for real hardcore sushi diners. Chopsticks are for sissies. If you do it, you'll impress everyone at the table."

"Will you do it with me?" she asked.

His blue eyes hardened. Rose got the impression he wasn't one to back down from a challenge.

"Sure, why not?" he said, and set his chopsticks back on the table.

Rose hesitated to use her fingers. But when Ethan picked up a roll, she was finally certain he wasn't joking. She followed his lead, raising one of her rolls halfway to her mouth.

"Cheers!" she said, bumping her California Maki into his before bravely putting the whole thing into her mouth.

"Cheers!" he responded, smiling.

After she'd tried a bite of everything he'd ordered for her, he said, "So, what's the verdict?"

Rose swallowed the last mouthful of the piece she was chewing. "To be honest, I've had better food..."

"Like a barbequed rack of greasy pork ribs?" he teased.

"Exactly. But I thought this would be a lot worse."

"So I haven't managed to bring you over to the raw side."

"I'm afraid not. Hey, I've been meaning to ask—what's this?" Rose pointed at a lime-green ball that looked like Play-Doh.

"That's wasabi."

"What's it for?"

"It adds a spicy flavor to the rolls."

"Oh, I like spicy food." She grabbed the ball.

"Don't," he warned. "It's really spicy."

She considered him for a second, the tiny ball still held between her thumb and index finger. *Okay, let's see...* Rose placed the tiny ball back on the wooden tablet acting as a plate and used one of her discarded chopsticks to split the wasabi into two identical halves.

"Is this better?" she asked.

He shook his head. "Not really, it's still too much."

"I can handle it."

Ethan was clearly trying and failing to suppress a grin as she raised the wasabi to her mouth. His expression said, *If you want to find out for yourself, I won't stop you.*

So it was a dare. Rose put the half ball in her mouth decided to win the challenge. But after gnawing for just a few seconds, her eyes started to water and her cheeks burned. Her nostrils flared wide as she tried to chew off the offending substance. She was sure she must look like a dragon breathing fire. To her credit, she managed to keep an almost straight face throughout the whole ordeal. When she finally managed to swallow the whole thing, she grabbed her diet Coke, shoved the straw aside, and downed the whole glass.

"Don't say anything," she hissed at Ethan once she could breathe again.

Rose needn't have admonished him as Ethan didn't seem able to talk. He was too busy laughing his head off.

When the dessert menu arrived, Rose disappeared behind it once again.

"Pssst," she whispered at Ethan a few moments later.

"You need help with the dessert?"

"No, thanks. I can figure out 'Green Tea Ice-Cream' all on my own. I wanted to ask you if there's something going on between you and that blonde chick." Rose jerked her chin toward the other end of the table. "The one sitting two seats down from Georgiana. She's been giving me a death stare all night."

"Ah, yes," Ethan admitted reluctantly. "That'd be Alice. We hooked up a couple of times, and now she probably thinks she's my girlfriend."

"Bah." Rose made a sarcastic swatting gesture with her hand. "How old-fashioned of her to think so."

So Ethan was a player, just like Tyler. But just how big of one? She quickly dismissed the train of thought; what did she care, anyway? Tonight had been a nice evening, sure—way more fun than she expected—but it wasn't as if they would see each other again after the dinner was over. So, player or not, it really made no difference to her.

Clink. Clink. Clink. Clink. Clink.

Georgiana was on her feet, looking down at all her guests, and batting a chopstick against her glass. The chatter quieted down, and twenty sets of eyes fixated on Georgiana. It was clear she loved being the center of attention. What was the big announcement, Rose wondered—a new Prada bag? A new Mercedes from Daddy?

"I wanted to thank you all for being here tonight for this special day…"

Oh, no. Her Birthday Majesty was really going to make a speech. Rose was about to roll her eyes at Ethan when she remembered he was Georgiana's brother and caught herself just in time.

"Tonight is special," Georgiana continued. "Not only because it's my birthday, but also because, as most of you already know"— Georgiana looked pointedly at Rose—"I won't be seeing you all for a few months, as I'm leaving in two weeks for France."

Did she say leaving? In two weeks? Going to *France*? *For months?*

Rose couldn't believe her luck. Georgiana out of the way meant one less complication for her and Tyler. She looked over at him, filled with hope and trepidation. But he'd gone very pale— he looked almost ill as he stared fixedly at the tablecloth. At that moment, as if sensing Rose's eyes on him, he lifted his head and looked at her from across the table. Rose knew that expression: guilt. Why? Georgiana moving to Europe was Christmas in August. So why the guilty face?

Rose's question was answered by the end of Georgiana's speech. "I couldn't believe my luck when Professor Hendricks told me there'd been a reshuffling in the semester abroad scholarship, and that Tyler and I would be able to join the program in the upcoming fall term! We're going to spend the next six months in Paris together! How exciting is that?" Georgiana addressed her question directly to Rose. As the table erupted in cheers and applause, Georgiana kept her gaze fixated on Rose, her lips twisted in a smug smile. Rose could practically feel the triumph wafting off her.

Despite the knife slicing deep into her heart, Rose didn't give Georgiana the satisfaction of crumbling right before her eyes. She managed to maintain an impassive expression on the outside—but inside?

Rose's brain whirled with thoughts. Her heart was pounding so fast she was afraid it'd escape her chest. Tyler was moving to Paris with his girlfriend, and he hadn't even bothered to tell her. A year ago, when he had applied for the program and lost the scholarship, Rose had been genuinely sorry. But now… she didn't want him to go. Rose hadn't bought Georgiana's explanation of a "reshuffling" in Hendricks's exchange program. He was one of the sternest, most revered professors at Harvard and didn't play favorites. Rose could only imagine what strings Georgiana's father must have pulled to get Tyler and his daughter in.

Whatever he'd done, it had worked. Tyler was leaving her. Rose felt the beginning of a sob forming in her throat, and choked it into her glass, pretending it was a hiccup.

Eleven

Ethan

Ethan watched Rose closely during Georgiana's speech. To the casual observer, she might have appeared unaffected by the news. But his scrutiny did not miss the flicker of hope on her face when Georgiana announced she was moving to France. In that moment, Rose's forehead lost all its creases, her eyes sparkled, and her mouth relaxed in a contented smile. It was only after Georgiana added that Tyler would be going with her that Rose's cheeks lost all their color and her expression soured, resembling the one she'd sported earlier while trying to swallow wasabi.

To her credit, Rose wasn't falling apart. At least not on the outside. She was sitting on her chair, staring ahead with a composed mask. Her fingers tapping on the table in a nervous tempo provided the only clue to her fury.

Interesting. So, Georgiana's she's-trying-to-steal-my-boyfriend theory wasn't paranoia. Something stronger than friendship linked Tyler to his attractive roommate. But from the pout of suppressed rage on Rose's lips, Ethan was sure

Gigi's move would crush their blossoming romance.

The icy stare Rose gave Tyler at the end of Georgiana's speech surprised Ethan. How quickly Rose's warm eyes could turn into a frosty wall of black steel when she was angry. He prayed he'd never be at the end of that stare. He felt almost sorry for Tyler. But, most of all, Ethan felt happy for himself. For once, Georgiana's scheming would prove quite useful. Rose fascinated him. It wasn't often these days that Ethan Smithson found a girl interesting. If he thought about it, it hadn't happened since Sabrina, and that had been a long time ago.

Georgiana

Outside the restaurant, Georgiana fidgeted with the fabric of her clutch, her jittery fingers picking a thread out of the floral embroidery. All the guests had left except for Tyler, Ethan, and Rose, who stood in the parking lot facing one another in an awkward circle.

Georgiana studied Rose's face for any sign of emotion. *Nothing.* She was just standing there looking annoyingly beautiful in her unusual clothes. In class, Rose wore a uniform of buttoned-to-the-neck shirts, pullovers, jeans, and flat boots. But tonight with her high heels and sexy jumpsuit, she was dressed to impress. Georgiana was sure Rose had dressed up to look good for her boyfriend.

The evening hadn't turned out as well as Georgiana had hoped. The stone-cold bitch had remained impassive throughout her speech. Had Tyler already told her about Paris? Georgiana couldn't be sure, one way or the other. Sometimes Rose was inscrutable. And her announcement tonight had not produced the powerful effect Georgiana anticipated, longed for. Rose crumbling in front of everybody or leaving the restaurant in a sobbing fit would've been the icing on her birthday cake. But it didn't really matter. In two weeks, Georgiana would be gone with Tyler, and Rose would no longer be a problem.

"Baby," Georgiana said to Tyler, linking arms with him. "Do you want to stay over at my place tonight?"

"Actually, I came here with Rose," Tyler said. "I should probably drive her home."

"Oh, I can do that," Ethan offered, stepping forward.

"I think it's better if I drive her home," Tyler said.

His possessive attitude irritated Georgiana. The day they left for France couldn't come fast enough.

"I'm sure Ethan is a proficient enough driver to see me home safely," Rose said, putting an end to the discussion. Her cold stare dared Tyler to add something.

Mmm. Well, well, well, look at that. Just when Georgiana thought her fun was spoiled, her moment of triumph had finally arrived. Rose was angry—*very* angry. Tyler hadn't told her about Paris after all. Georgiana made an evil laugh inside her head. *Muahahah, mission accomplished.*

"It's all set, then," Georgiana chirped, moving toward Tyler's car.

It was annoying for her brother to pay attention to Rose tonight since he didn't have to anymore. Not to say mortifying for the way he'd ignored her sorority little sister, Alice. From what Alice had told her, she and her brother were in a committed relationship. So why flirt with another girl all night and offer to take her home? Especially now that Georgiana didn't need him involved with Rose. Anyway, if her brother wanted to toy with Rose, whatever. The more water under the bridge of Rose and Tyler, the better. But poor Alice.

"I'm this way," Ethan said, steering Rose away with a hand on the small of her back.

Georgiana pulled Tyler toward his car and tried to ignore the fact that her boyfriend appeared jealous of her brother.

Twelve

Rose

Ethan drove a black Mercedes SL—a sports car that fitted his character like a glove. Rose was glad it was *him* driving her home tonight. The thought of being stuck in a confined space with Tyler was unbearable just now. She didn't even care that he was staying over at Georgiana's. She was too angry for that.

They didn't speak much on the way to Tyler's house, except for Rose offering the occasional direction. All the playfulness of the night had evaporated, and with too much on her mind to make small talk, Rose kept quiet. Ethan didn't seem to mind the silence, though.

When they pulled up in front of Tyler's building, Ethan was jumping out of the car before Rose even had a chance to thank him for driving her home. He circled it to reach her side and opened the car door for her. A tiny smile escaped her lips; this guy was full of surprises.

"How gentlemanly of you," she said, taking his outstretched hand.

"I'm no gentlemen," he said, his eyes suddenly dark in the cold night. "I only wanted to do this."

Ethan pulled her up and out of the car toward him. Moving his free hand to the small of her back and forcing their bodies closer together, he kissed her.

At first, she turned rigid in his arms. Rose hadn't expected the kiss, but after the initial surprise, she found herself responding. Her body took control, and she pressed herself against him. As suddenly as she'd let herself go, though, Rose regained control and pulled away from him.

She threw him a quick glance, blushing. Rose's eyes traveled low, fixating on the curb for a while before she was steady enough to look at him again.

Leaning with her back against his car, she said, "I guess that was good night, then."

"I guess it was."

"Good night, Ethan." Rose stepped toward him.

"Good night, Rose." He cupped her face in his hands and planted a soft kiss on her lips.

Rose could sense his stare on her back as she walked away, and couldn't resist glancing back at him one last time. Ethan had taken her place against his car, watching her go, his gaze smoldering. Rose ran the last few steps toward the door and disappeared inside the house, feeling out of breath.

The moment she closed the door, however, the brief elation Ethan's kiss had given her vanished. As she collapsed to the floor, a strong pain constricted her lungs. Rose rested her head on her knees and let the tears she'd been holding back for the past hour run freely.

Tyler

In Georgiana's apartment, in her bed, Tyler lay awake, restless. Georgiana was sleeping naked beside him, snoring faintly. He'd had sex with her tonight, more out of frustration than anything else. Tyler hadn't enjoyed it; he'd been thinking about Rose the entire time. Even when she wasn't here, she was all he could think about. He'd been livid with her all night for the way she'd openly flirted with Georgiana's brother. And now, white-hot jealousy was coursing through his veins like venom.

Tyler couldn't get the image of her going home with Ethan out of his mind. Had she really gone home, or had she gone back to his apartment? Was she having sex with him now? The thought of Rose, naked, with somebody else was unbearable. Unthinkable. The image was enough to send him shooting out of the bed. Tyler needed to know,

now. He had to know if she was at home, waiting for him or not.

The sudden movement woke Georgiana. She stirred and looked at him. The room was in half-darkness; the only light came from the street lamps outside. Tyler doubted she could see much more of him than his dark silhouette.

"What's up, baby?" she asked.

"I can't sleep. I need my bed."

"You never had a problem with my bed before."

"I do tonight," he said harshly. Then, realizing it'd be easier to be nice to Georgiana rather than start an argument, he leaned toward her to kiss her forehead. "I'll call you tomorrow when I wake up, okay? Now, go back to sleep."

Apparently soothed by his sweet tone, Georgiana didn't protest further, her eyelids fluttering shut.

The journey home seemed infinite to Tyler, even though the streets were deserted this late at night. Every red light seemed to linger for an eternity. He sat in his car nervously drumming his fingers on the wheel, coils of anxiety twisting his stomach into knots. Rose was home, she had to be home. Tyler needed to explain Paris to her, and then she'd forgive him. Rose always did. Six months was nothing. They'd known each other for all their lives; six months in France didn't matter.

When he finally pulled over in front of his house, Tyler parked the car in a hurry and ran up the alleyway. Once inside, he paused briefly in the entrance hall, listening for any sound. Nothing. All was silent. He took off his shoes and jacket without turning on any lights and ran up the stairs, trying not to make too much noise.

Rose's door was closed. He stopped in front of it for a moment, undecided. But he had to know. He turned the knob slowly, again careful not to produce a sound.

Tyler peered into the room, filled with trepidation. The lights were all off, and the curtains closed. But his eyes were already used to the semi-darkness, and he could distinguish the slim outline of a body lying on the bed, curled up under the covers.

Rose was home. Of course, she was home. Relief washed over him. How stupid had he been to think she would've gone home with that dude? Rose loved him. She'd be angry with him in the morning, sure, and would probably yell at him, but she'd always be there for him. Tyler went to bed, the most relaxed he'd been the entire week. Everything would be fine.

Thirteen

Rose

Rose cried herself to sleep and woke up the next morning feeling miserable. A few groggy seconds passed before Rose remembered why she was in such a terrible mood. *Tyler was moving to France with Georgiana.* At the thought, her stomach churned and Rose pressed her lips together trying not to gag. What now? She'd have to move out at once. The realization made her even angrier; in one swift move, Georgiana was going to get everything she wanted. Rose hated her like she'd never hated anyone in her entire life.

Her loathing of Georgiana was interrupted by the sound of the toilet being flushed. Tyler was home. Rose's heart skipped a beat. When had he returned? What was the time? 7:45. What was Tyler doing home so early? Rose couldn't talk to him, not a mere few hours after learning the truth of where she stood with him. In fact, her plan was to sneak out of the house before he got back from Georgiana's place and return long after his bedtime. What was she going to do now? Rose wasn't ready to face him. She didn't want to see him at all.

Her heart felt like it stopped altogether when a faint knock sounded on her door. *Shoot! What now?* Rose didn't move. She didn't breathe.

The knock came again, louder this time. A shiver ran down Rose's spine and she lifted the covers higher over her head as if they could shield her from Tyler.

"Rose?" Tyler's voice came tentatively from the other side. "Rose, I know you're in there."

How did he know?

"Rose, we need to talk."

Oh, so now he wants to talk.

"Go away!" she shouted, jerking out of bed. No chance of being embarrassed as she was wearing a baggy T-shirt and long pajama pants.

"Rose, I'm coming in."

Tyler came into the room, dressed in a white T-shirt and gray sweat pants.

"I don't want to talk to you," she said.

They faced each other, standing on opposite sides of her bed.

"Rose, please, I had no choice."

She'd expected this excuse and was ready for it. "Oh, really?" Rose snapped. "And what exactly stopped you from telling me you were moving to France with your girlfriend?"

"That's not what I meant."

"Why didn't you tell me? *Why*?" Rose yelled, hysterical. "Oh, yeah! Because you wanted to keep screwing me until you left. You're a jerk."

"Rose, please, it's not like that and you know it. I wasn't expecting any of this to happen. Professor Hendricks summoned me into his office last Monday to tell me Montgomery had backed out of the French scholarship and that, if I wanted it, the spot was mine. But since the program started in three weeks, I had to give him an answer right then—and you know how much I wanted that scholarship. So, I said yes. I didn't even know Georgiana was also going until I'd already accepted."

"That witch made this happen, didn't she? *How*?" Rose could hear the venom in her voice, but she didn't care.

"I don't know. Both Montgomery and Brown withdrew from the exchange program at the last second. Georgiana must've had her father involved—I'm guessing he offered them something to give up their spots."

"Did you sleep with her?" Rose hissed.

"What?" Tyler seemed thrown off balance by the fury of her question.

"Last night. Did. You. Have. Sex. With. *Her*?"

It was the first time Rose asked him, and she had a hunch it was also the wrong time to ask.

Tyler looked at her with a desperate expression.

"You bastard…" Rose started to sob.

"Rose, please, it didn't mean anything. I was thinking about you the entire time."

How many times had she heard that same plea? Every time he'd cheated on one of his girlfriends and had been caught…

Oh, no. She'd become one of his girls. The thing she'd feared the most had become true.

"Get out," she commanded. "I don't want to talk to you. I don't even want to see you."

"Rose, please…"

"Get out."

"Rose…"

"I said GET OUT!" she screamed.

Tyler

Tyler had never seen Rose this mad, and to be honest, she was scaring him a little. So he did as she asked and gave her space, resolving to talk to her later, once she calmed down.

He never got the chance. In the next few days, Rose became a ghost. She left the house at dawn and always came back after midnight. When he waited up for her, Rose ran from the entrance door to her room, ignoring his calls as she locked herself inside. One night he camped outside her bedroom, determined to catch her before she left the next morning. But he fell asleep on the floor as he kept vigil. When Tyler awoke the next morning, Rose was gone. She must've stepped over his sleeping body and left without waking him. Even outside the house, he couldn't find a chance to talk to her—Georgiana shadowed him everywhere, and he was never alone long enough to seek Rose out.

During his last week in the States, Rose disappeared altogether, only to reappear two days before he was to leave for Paris. Tyler suspected she'd gone home to Dallas to visit her family without telling him.

The night before his departure, Tyler was in his room, finishing packing, when he heard the front door slam shut. Rose was home; no one else had a key. For a moment, he was tempted to go out and try to talk to her again. But given how badly every previous attempt had gone, he decided it was better to wait until he was back from France. When Tyler returned, he'd get rid of Georgiana, and then Rose would forgive him.

Fourteen

Rose

Rose hid in her room, feeling dead inside. Tyler was leaving tomorrow; he wouldn't just be in a different city, he'd be on a different continent entirely. She'd done her best to avoid him after their fight. Rose didn't want to hear his excuses; she'd heard all of them before. The same words uttered a thousand times to as many girls. When she'd found him sleeping outside her door, she'd almost given in, but somehow she'd managed to stay strong.

But tonight was different. It was their last night.

Rose changed into one of the longish T-shirts she liked to use to sleep and lay on the bed, but she couldn't stand still. On impulse, she got up, crossed the hall, and burst Tyler's door open. He was already in bed, his hand halfway to the table lamp, ready to turn it off.

Tyler looked up at Rose, surprised. "Oh, so now you're talking to me?" he asked.

"No," she said, removing her T-shirt in one swift movement. "Not talking."

***

Afterward, Rose spent the night awake on the bed, staring at the black ceiling and listening to Tyler's deep breathing as he slept beside her. When she got scared he might wake up, she snuck out of the bed. Outside his window, the first light of dawn was approaching, and the night fled before it. Just like Rose was fleeing from Tyler.

She collected her discarded T-shirt from the floor and tiptoed toward the safety of her room. Once inside, Rose locked the door. Tyler wouldn't try to wake her the next morning; he had to leave early for the airport. She didn't want to say goodbye. She couldn't.

***

Over the next few weeks, the memory of that night haunted Rose, no matter how much she tried to push it out of her mind. She needed to forget Tyler. He was in Paris with Georgiana. What were they doing? No, no, no. She had to stop torturing herself obsessing over what Tyler was or wasn't doing and move on.

A six-month break would do the trick. It had to. If she wanted things to go back to the way they'd been, she only needed time to forgive and forget. It wasn't too late for them to be friends again. But she needed to move out before he came back; this house was too full of him, too full of them.

Right, *move*. It was a Saturday morning, three weeks after Tyler and Georgiana had left. Rose was at the kitchen table scrolling through Craigslist, looking for rental houses. She'd already found a few options within her price range, but the pictures were so revolting that the search was doing nothing to improve her mood.

As she looked at one ugly house picture after another, her phone started ringing. An unknown number beginning with the Boston area code appeared on-screen.

"Hello?" she greeted, perplexed. It wasn't often she received phone calls from unknown numbers.

"Rose?"

It was a male voice, one she didn't recognize.

"Yes? Who is this?"

"You have no idea who I am. Ouch, I'm hurt."

He was funny, and she liked his voice, but she kept quiet.

"It's Ethan."

Her stomach did a little flip.

"Georgiana's brother," he added for good measure.

Georgiana. Tyler. France. Her stomach landed from the flip with an almighty crash.

"Oh, hi," she said, trying to keep an even tone. It wasn't easy; she felt like she might start sobbing at any moment.

"Hi." He sounded put-off by her subdued reply—which, somehow, uplifted her.

She resumed in a much cheerier tone. "Just when I thought you'd forgotten all about me." She had a hunch it wasn't by chance he'd waited until Tyler was out of the country before calling her.

"Well, I had to make sure I could present a winner before calling you."

"A winner?" Rose asked, both puzzled and captivated.

"I have a wager to propose."

"This early on a Saturday morning? Shouldn't we wait until at least, I don't know, late afternoon before we start gambling?"

"Normally I'd say yes, but since I have a better chance of winning in broad daylight, you'll have to make an exception."

"Would I want you to win?" she asked, surprised by her own coquettishness.

"I think it'll be a win-win, so yeah…"

"Mmm, I'm intrigued. Tell me everything."

An hour later, as she walked up the steps of a fancy new building just a few blocks away from

Harvard, she knew she'd lost the bet. As Ethan had predicted, she was not at all sorry about her defeat.

Ethan had called to show her an apartment he thought she might like on the condition that if she were to take it, she'd have to go out to dinner with him. Rose vaguely remembered telling him about her search for an apartment the night of Georgiana's party. It hadn't been true back then, and she hadn't foreseen her lie becoming the truth quite so abruptly. But now she was glad for it. She welcomed the distraction; it was the first positive thing that had happened to her in a while.

Ethan had picked her up in his black Mercedes thirty minutes after calling her. She'd barely had time to take a quick shower and get dressed before he'd arrived.

"Are you sure this is within my budget?" she asked, eying the luxurious building.

"The owner's a good friend of mine, and he's agreed to lower the price for a reliable, tidy tenant who won't trash the place," Ethan explained shrugging. "A lot of rich, spoiled frat boys want to live here, but they're trying to keep them out of the building and make it more of an adult community."

"How do you know I'm not a crazy party girl?"

"Are you?" Ethan called her bluff.

"No," she admitted, unsettled by the x-raying of his light blue eyes.

"Shall we?" he asked, holding the door open for her.

The apartment was perfect, just perfect. It was a spacious one-bedroom with one wall made entirely of floor-to-ceiling windows. The kitchen was ultra-modern, brand new, and had a huge island that overlooked the dining table and part of the living room. The bedroom was bigger than the one Rose was occupying now and had a walk-in closet. Even the bathroom was cozy with all-new counters and sinks, and furnished in a minimal style that suited the place. Both the furniture and walls were painted white with splashes of warm gray and wood accents.

Compared to what was on Craigslist, this place was a palace. Rose could hardly believe her luck.

"Do I take it we have a date?" Ethan asked when she was finished examining every inch of the apartment.

"When can I move in?" she asked, beaming.

"Next weekend. I'll have you sign some papers, and it's a done deal."

"You don't need to check with the owner?"

"Nah, I had you pre-approved."

"Confident, are we?"

He smiled dashingly.

"When do you want to go out?" Ethan asked once the paperwork was taken care of.

"You're the winner, you call the shots."

"Next Friday?"

Something dangerous fluttered in Rose's belly. "Next Friday it is," she said.

Fifteen

Rose

In the following days, Rose changed her mind about how she felt about going out with Ethan every other hour. At first, she'd be happy for the distraction. Then she'd get worried about getting into even bigger trouble. Ethan was another bad boy, possibly even worse than Tyler. Why couldn't she find one of the good ones?

Because you find them boring as hell, a nasty little voice replied in Rose's head.

When she was done worrying about how much Ethan might hurt her, guilt towards Tyler crept in, even though she knew she shouldn't feel anything but anger about the situation. After all, Tyler was in Paris with his girlfriend. But her heart was stupid, and it kept telling Rose she was being disloyal. Once the guilt trip was over, Rose switched almost immediately to vindictiveness— of all the guys she could have gone out with, Ethan would definitely annoy Tyler the most.

Not that he'd find out considering they barely talked these days. She'd emailed him once to say she was moving out, and that she'd check on his house every now and then, and pay the bills while he was in France. But Tyler hadn't emailed her back, probably because he almost never checked his non-Harvard email account. And she was perfectly happy with him not knowing, at least for a while, until she had enough time to settle into her new place—and life, hopefully.

Ethan was due to pick her up at 7:00 pm. It was 6:30, and Rose was already dressed. She had chosen her clothes for tonight well in advance as everything else was packed away in two huge suitcases for her big move tomorrow. She'd opted for a casual-chic style: a white neoprene quilted sweater over lightly faded ultra-skinny jeans and a pair of high-heeled nude pumps. In front of the mirror, Rose let her hair down and styled it in soft waves. As for makeup, she kept it simple: foundation, bronze blush, a double coat of mascara, and lip balm. Rose didn't like to wear lipstick or lip-gloss at restaurants. She didn't see the point when it would just end up on a napkin by the end of the night.

At 6:55, the doorbell rang. Rose unhooked her black fur jacket from its hanger and hurried out of the house to meet Ethan.

He drove to a fancy steak house for their first official date—he'd remembered meat was her favorite. She added one point for him in her mental scoreboard.

"I wish I'd given in to Georgiana sooner," Ethan said after they'd drunk their first glass of wine.

"Meaning?" Rose asked, uneasy at the mention of Georgiana. She tried to store the notion of her being Ethan's sister in a remote corner of her brain.

"She's been bugging me to go out with you for ages," Ethan explained.

"How nice of her to worry about me," Rose said, unable to keep the sarcasm out of her voice. Anger at Georgiana's scheming resurfaced immediately.

"I don't think she was being utterly altruistic," Ethan said. He was direct; Rose liked it. "I guess she was jealous of you and Tyler living together."

Tyler's name made Rose blush. She hoped the reaction wasn't too obvious, even if Ethan's attentive stare told her otherwise.

"So what made you change your mind?" Rose asked, steering the conversation away from Tyler. She didn't want to think about him tonight.

"I met you," Ethan said simply, holding her gaze.

He meant it to be a charming statement, but suspicion flared in Rose's chest at once. "So what is this?" She wiggled a finger between them. "A favor you're doing your sister?"

"Ah, no. Miss Atwood, your accusations wound me."

"Please be square with me." Rose broke the courting act. She was tired of guys playing games. "Are you here only because Georgiana asked you?"

Ethan's ever-present lopsided smile disappeared. "I would never do that," he said. "I'm here because I want to be. I'm here because the night I met you was the first night I'd had fun in forever. And because I hope that by the end of the night you'll let me kiss you again."

"Okay." Rose swallowed. When Ethan Smithson switched on the charm, he was impossible to resist. Maybe she really was jumping head first into bigger trouble. "Let's not talk about other people then."

Ethan nodded just as the server was arriving to take their orders.

The rest of the night passed in a blur of general getting-to-know-you talk. Rose found she was able to relax with Ethan; he had an easy way about things, quite the opposite of his snotty sister, and he made her laugh—a lot! He didn't mention Tyler again during the dinner, much to Rose's relief. Besides her asking, Rose suspected Ethan was avoiding the topic so as not to spoil their first date. Deep down, Rose feared the moment she'd have to come clean about her relationship with Tyler. If she wanted to keep seeing Ethan, she'd have to tell him the ugly truth eventually. How would Ethan react? Would he hate her for hurting his sister? Think of her as the other woman?

When Ethan pulled up in front of Tyler's house, Rose was surprised to see the clock of his car read 1:00 a.m.

"Do you need any help with the big move tomorrow?" Ethan asked.

"Yeah, sure, I'll stick my humongous luggage in your spacious trunk," she joked, wondering if his sports car even had a trunk.

"I'll have you know I'm also equipped with a pickup, Miss Atwood. It should be more than capable of hauling your humongous luggage."

She'd planned to call a cab, but the possibility of Ethan helping her was far more enticing.

"Okay then. But only if you'll let me buy you breakfast afterwards."

"Deal," he said.

"Should we shake on it?"

"I have a better idea," he said, and leaned in to kiss her.

***

"You seem undecided," Ethan said.

They'd just finished moving Rose's luggage into her new apartment, and Rose was famished.

"Well," Rose said, shifting her gaze between the two sides of the road. "I love Starbucks' coffee, but I prefer donuts from Dunkin' Donuts."

All night she'd thought about Ethan. About their date the night before, the conversations they'd had, the occasional fluttering in her belly, and the kiss! Yesterday had been the first night Tyler had not haunted her dreams.

"You get the coffee, and I'll get the donuts," Ethan proposed.

"But breakfast was supposed to be on me!" Rose protested.

He laughed. "So pay me back the two dollars the donuts will cost."

Rose smiled and gave in. "Okay. Let's meet back here and we can eat in my new kitchen."

***

"Do you ever miss Texas?" Ethan asked her as they ate breakfast seated at Rose's new table next to the wall-wide windows. Sunlight filtered through the glass, making her new apartment appear even brighter than when she'd seen it the first time.

"Sometimes, but we moved here seven years ago, so now Boston feels like home too," Rose said.

"You keep saying *we*."

"Ah," Rose said, embarrassed. "Bad habit."

"Any other bad habits I should know of?"

Ethan's question was vague enough, but the is-there-something-going-on-between-you-and-Tyler subtext was all too clear.

"Who am I talking to?" Rose asked. "Georgiana's brother or just Ethan?"

"Just Ethan," he replied, and somehow Rose trusted him.

"Tyler is my best friend; we managed to stay *just* friends for a long time."

"Past tense?"

"Past tense," she confirmed.

Ethan didn't press her; he waited for her to tell him more, or not tell him anything. This made her even more confident she could open up to him, and she did. Rose told him everything; she started with Marcus and ended with the disaster the last couple of months had been.

"...and now you probably hate me because Georgiana is your sister and I've been horrible to her."

"I don't hate you," Ethan said, though he'd gone rigid in his chair. "I know my sister's not an angel, but she doesn't deserve to be cheated on. Still, I'm not angry at you—how could I be? You weren't the one cheating on Georgiana. Tyler's the bastard who was playing both of you like that. He's lucky he's on another continent!"

Rose's cheeks were beyond red at this point. "Do you think she knows?" she asked, not daring to look him in the eye.

"From what Gigi told me, she's almost certain."

"And she doesn't care?"

"My sister's peculiar like that," Ethan said noncommittally. "Georgiana has decided she wants to be with Tyler, and as long as she gets what she wants, she doesn't seem to care if he wants to be with her or not."

"So you don't hate me for hurting her? Are you sure?"

"As I said, you aren't the one who's in the wrong here. That Tyler dude, though—him, I hate. I could snap his neck. Do you love him?"

"I do," Rose said sincerely. "But I'm not sure if I'm *in* love with him. Our relationship is too complicated to trace a line where the friendship ends and the love starts. But what we did was a huge mistake, and I hope we can find our way back to being just friends. What about you? Anyone I should know about?"

"Not really…"

"What about that blonde girl at Georgiana's birthday?" *The one glaring at me*, Rose silently added. "What was her name?"

"Alice."

"Alice, right. Are you still seeing her?"

Ethan shrugged.

Meaning, yes.

"The night we met, did you go see her after you dropped me off?" Rose pressed.

Ethan's eyebrows flew upward; he was clearly taken aback by the question. "I did," he admitted.

"Did you sleep together?"

Ethan replied with a curt nod, his jaw tense.

"And after that?"

Another small nod.

"When was the last time?"

"Two nights before our date."

"Will there be a next?" Rose asked, not sure she wanted to know.

"I don't know," Ethan answered honestly.

"Listen." Rose took a sip of her coffee, which had gone cold. "I genuinely like you…"

"I sense a 'but' coming," Ethan said with a skeptical smile.

"But… I don't want to be mixed up in another love triangle. My life is already too complicated as is. I don't want to fool around. And let's not kid ourselves—you're Georgiana's brother. That's not irrelevant."

"You're right," Ethan said. He stood up and pulled on his black leather jacket. "I should sort myself out first." He moved toward the door.

"If you ever do, well, you know where I live." Rose followed him to the door and held it open for him.

"Goodbye, Miss Atwood." Ethan kissed her on the forehead.

Rose liked that he acted like a gentleman out of a Jane Austen novel whenever he was flirting. "Goodbye, Mr. Smithson," she said, playing along.

She watched Ethan go and closed the door behind him, leaning her forehead against the cold metal. Rose was already feeling a pang of regret. Had she done the right thing? If so, then why the disappointment?

Because doing the right thing sucked, she answered herself. But she'd done enough wrong for a while, and she wanted her next relationship to start out clean. No secrets, no sneaking around, and most definitely no other women. If the bare mention of an exclusive relationship sent Ethan running for the hills, it'd be even clearer she'd made the right choice.

Sixteen

Rose

Once she was settled into her new home, Rose started settling into her new, independent life as well. Being out of Tyler's house helped more than she'd expected. Not having to see him or Georgiana was the icing on her recovery cake. Six months was a long break. By the time Tyler came back, her heart would be healed, and she'd be in control of her feelings once again. Really, France was the perfect solution, and the only way to salvage her friendship with Tyler.

This forced break was the longest they'd ever been apart, but Rose didn't have time to feel alone. Harvard Law was more than enough to keep her mind busy, and without distractions her grades had become even better than usual. Rose was concentrating on herself and on her studies. She was alone, independent, in control of her life... and it felt good.

***

Rose stretched in bed, half asleep. It was Saturday morning and even if she had to study, she hadn't set the alarm clock. Unexpectedly, the doorbell rang, cutting her morning treat short.

Rose stared at the ceiling, confused for a few seconds. It must be the mailman delivering her latest textbook order. She reluctantly shuffled out of bed, adjusted her hair in a messy bun, and went to open the door wearing only her pale gray just-above-the-knee nightdress and a pair of socks. She had a paper to write anyway, so the delivery was as good a wake-up call as any.

But there wasn't a mailman waiting for her on her landing. Rather, it was Ethan, holding a tray of coffee cups and a box of donuts.

"Trick or treat?" he asked.

"Aren't you supposed to wear a costume for that?" Rose said groggily, her voice still thick with sleep. She'd forgotten it was Halloween.

"Not a morning person, huh?" Ethan said with a wicked smile.

"Guilty."

"Don't you even want to know the plea bargain first?"

"You have donuts in one hand and coffee in the other. I'm good." Rose smiled. "Come on in. Let me go put something on."

"No, please, it's the first time I've seen your legs. They look too good to be covered up."

"Well, sorry, but I'm not comfortable being the only one in the room not wearing pants."

"In that case…" In a swift move, Ethan dropped everything on the kitchen table and kicked away his shoes. He was already unbuttoning his pants before Rose realized what he was doing.

"That's not what I meant!" she protested, covering her face with her hands. But he was already folding his pants neatly in two. Ethan laid the pants on the back of a chair on which he sat afterwards. Rose had no choice left other than to sit opposite him and try to ignore the fact that there was a half-naked, very attractive guy sitting in her kitchen.

"So what brings you to this part of town?" Rose sipped her coffee, pleased to notice he'd remembered she loved cappuccinos.

"Oh, I like to check on tenants I've helped find a place for from time to time."

"You mean you bring coffee and donuts to all of them?"

"No, donuts are a special perk I reserve for you."

"I'm honored." She took a bite to show her appreciation.

"You've been all right, then? You have all you need?"

Rose knew his question wasn't a casual one, but she gave him a casual answer all the same. "I'm missing something red."

"Red?"

"Yeah, I like the minimalist style, but I need a pop of color."

"Don't tell me you have an artistic side! So un-lawyer-like of you. How's everything else been?"

"Same old. You know, I'm having fun with Constitutional Law." Rose knew she was avoiding his questions, but she wasn't sure what he was doing here yet. "How about you?"

"I've pretty much been a lone wolf for the last month."

He looked a bit like a wolf—one with piercing blue eyes.

"Not on my account, I hope?" Rose hid her face behind her coffee cup.

"To be honest, Miss Atwood, it has been on your account."

Rose smiled. She really liked when he acted the gentleman. "You want more coffee?"

"Sure."

She moved into the kitchen and Ethan sprawled out on the couch. Rose had almost forgotten he was pants-less. Watching Ethan Smithson wander around her living room in boxer shorts was weird and thrilling at the same time.

"Just coffee, or do you want a cappuccino?" she asked from behind the kitchen island.

"You make cappuccinos at home?"

"Yeah, I have a frothing machine."

"Then a cappuccino."

Rose brought two huge mugs to the couch and sat opposite Ethan, draping her calves on his lap. For a horrible moment, Rose feared she'd forgotten to shave her legs, before remembering she'd done it last night. *Phew*.

"Is this what your typical Saturday morning looks like?"

"Nah, I'm usually caught up in boring stuff like accounting or supervising some remodeling project. Running a company is a 24/7 job. And being a grownup isn't fun."

"I wouldn't know about that. I'm still in grad-school limbo. And I have at least another year before I have to grow up."

"Lucky you."

"So what were you like as a kid, before you went over to the grownups side?"

"I was a little terror…"

Rose chuckled. "I can imagine that."

"I drove my mom and sisters crazy, but they adored me all the same."

"Sisters, plural?"

"Yeah, Georgiana is the youngest. Victoria—Vicky—is the middle kid, and I'm the oldest."

"I didn't know you had another sister. Georgiana never mentioned her, and she wasn't at her birthday."

"That's weird because they're tight as hell. I'm sure Vicky didn't make it to Gigi's party because she was stuck in an office with a big case to work on. Ever since I quit the practice, Vicky's career has been my father's consolation. She puts eighty to ninety hours a week into the family business, and she's even engaged to another pedigreed lawyer. They're getting married next year, and I'm sure they'll breed another generation of perfect little lawyers. She's a daughterly dream come true. Despite that, I love her. Vick manages to remain human even after going over to the Dark Side."

"You really can't stand lawyers. Should I remind you I'm going to be one pretty soon?"

"I won't hold it against you, I promise."

"So you never liked law?"

Ethan shrugged. "In school, I didn't mind it per se. It was more the fact of not having a choice that didn't sit well with me. To do it just because I was supposed to, expected to. And yes, I hated staying all those hours in the office, but running a company isn't that different. I have to be on the job just as much, but since it's my choice, I'm happy about it. Does that make any sense?"

"It makes a lot of sense."

"And being a lawyer still has its perks. I don't need anyone to draft my contracts, which saves me a lot of money. What about you? Have you always wanted to be a lawyer?"

"Yeah, my dad passed it on to me. He wanted to be a lawyer, but couldn't."

"Couldn't?"

"My grandparents both died in a car accident right after he graduated from college. He'd already been accepted to Harvard Law, but couldn't go. His brother and sister were still young—my uncle, Adam, was in high school and Aunt Debra was even younger. My dad had to go back home to take care of them."

"I'm sorry."

"Thank you, but it's okay. It was a long time ago. Anyway, when my dad moved back to Dallas, he took over the family business and provided for his brother and sister. He was already engaged to my mom, so dad became their stepfather and mom their stepmother, sort of. By the time my aunt and uncle were old enough to take care of themselves, I was already three and the company was doing well. With a daughter and a wife to care for, my dad didn't want to leave a secure position to follow his dream, but he kept studying on his own. He'd discuss cases and sentences with me when I became old enough. We always watched crime shows together, judging the cases they presented. And we loved playing court or just discussing this or that sentence."

"No dolls and fairy tales for you?"

Rose chuckled. "No, only vicious crimes. Anyway, Dad was so passionate about it that he passed on his love of the law to me, and I absorbed it like a sponge. It's what I wrote in my admission paper to Harvard Law; in fact, I think it was one of the main reasons I was accepted into the program. So yeah, I've always wanted to be a lawyer."

"I should introduce you to my dad. He'd probably want to adopt you right away," Ethan commented with a dashing smile.

He really is a terror, Rose thought. *A dangerously attractive one*. She tried to speak with an even tone when she asked her next question, the one she'd been burning to ask since he'd arrived. "So you've gone solitary just for me, huh? May I ask why?"

"You've piqued my interest, Miss Atwood."

"How so?"

"For one, you look adorable with a foam mustache." Ethan leaned in to wipe it away with his thumb. *Uh-oh, too close*, she thought. And then he was kissing her.

Rose let herself melt into the kiss, even knowing she shouldn't trust Ethan. She'd done some asking around in Georgiana's inner circle of friends, and they'd all confirmed he was a big player. But even against her better judgment, she felt secure in his arms. So she let him drop their mugs on her coffee table, and she let herself go without thinking, without being in control... and it felt even better.

Seventeen

Ethan

"You look worried," Ethan said, watching Rose dress herself self-consciously hiding behind the couch. He couldn't help thinking she was even more adorable when she frowned.

"I was just wondering if you were going to give me the speech now."

"Meaning?"

Ethan snatched his pants, pulled them on, and started buttoning up his shirt.

"I ran a background check on you, Mr. Smithson," Rose said. "You have quite a reputation."

"Ah, Miss Atwood, you don't do me justice." He flashed Rose his most dashing grin. "What falsehoods have you heard?"

"That you pretty much run away from relationships the minute they become serious."

Ethan's smile evaporated. "I don't like to waste anyone's time."

"Is that so?" Rose's face darkened.

Ethan sat at the kitchen table, undecided on what to say. True, he hadn't had a serious relationship in forever, not since… *Sabrina*. In part, because he had yet to meet someone who really interested him. In part, it had been his fault. Ethan had bolted from a number of relationships because they were becoming too serious, just like Rose said. It had been too soon after Sabrina. But now? Was he finally ready to move on? Could he open up with Rose? Bare his heart to her? He'd never told anyone about what had really happened with Sabrina. The official version for everyone— relatives, including Ethan's parents, and friends— had been cold feet. And even if Ethan's mom suspected the truth, only his sisters knew the story firsthand.

Rose followed him into the kitchen and braced her hands on the back of a chair. "Come on," she prompted. "I don't judge. Plus, you're obliged to tell me."

"And why is that?"

"Because I've already confessed my darkest secrets to you. And if you tell me about those closet skeletons, I'll feed you."

"Feed me what?" Ethan said.

Rose opened a cupboard and studied its insides. "How does boxed mac and cheese sound?"

"Perfect." Despite himself, Ethan smiled again. Rose was so un-domestic it was endearing. "If you throw in a beer, we have a deal."

Rose put the pasta on the stove to cook and sat in front of him, placing two bottles of Coors Light on the table. No glasses—Ethan liked her style. He liked it even more when she laid the head of the bottle on the edge of the table and punched the cap loose.

Ethan chuckled. "That's a handy skill."

"Dorm-earned skills," Rose joked.

"I don't want to know." Ethan really didn't; thinking of Rose in a college dorm made him jealous. He was already becoming territorial and didn't like just how much.

Rose smiled, passed him the opened bottle, and repeated the procedure with the other. Once done, she lifted the second bottle in a "cheers" gesture, and said, "Mr. Smithson, you owe me a story."

"Would you rather have the short or long version?"

Rose studied him, took a sip of beer, and said, "Short, please."

"Her name was Sabrina, and we were engaged. Not a distant future thing, we had the whole marriage shenanigans going. Booked venue, sent invitations, she had a dress…" Ethan winced at the memory. "Anyway, one sorry evening three months before the wedding, I came home early and found her in bed with the best man. Bit cliché, I know." Ethan hid his pain behind sarcasm. "Now they're married. They moved to New York about two years ago."

"I'm sorry," Rose whispered.

"No need to be. It was a long time ago. But now it takes me a little longer to commit to anything or anyone. When a girl starts talking rings after three dates, I tell her I'm not marriage material and we usually part ways."

"That's so cynical."

"More fair."

"So where does this leave us?"

"Not sure what you're asking." Ethan shrugged. "Where do you want it to leave us?"

"Here's what I think." Rose scrunched her face, trying to order her thoughts. "I'm tired of investing in relationships and people who walk out on me. I'm not saying we should define anything today. I only want to know that if we start going out, and if things get serious, you won't bolt just because. Do you think you can keep an open mind?"

"I think your mac and cheese is burning."

Rose threw herself at the pot to salvage whatever was left of the pasta. Not much from the smell of it.

"It's ruined." She sighed, turning towards him.

Ethan stood up and wrapped his arms around her waist. "How about I take you out to lunch?"

Rose tilted her face upward and her beautiful dark eyes met his. "And where would you take me?"

Her question had nothing to do with food. Neither did his answer. "You can trust me."

FOUR MONTHS LATER

Eighteen

Tyler

Tyler was nervous, edgy as he walked up the steps of Rose's new building. He hadn't called her to tell her he'd stop by—heck, she probably didn't even know he was back from France. He'd deliberately chosen not to give her warning. What if Rose refused to see him? Tyler couldn't wait a minute longer. One night home without her had been enough.

When his plane landed, he had to use all his self-control not to go to Rose in the middle of the night the moment he set foot in the US. Instead, Tyler had settled for leaving home super early the next morning. As he reached the building entrance, a chill wind blew on him from behind, the air even crisper than usual for January in Boston.

Tyler warmed his clenched fists by puffing hot air into them and opened the heavy door. He searched the hall for the elevators. Rose should be on the second floor, apartment 2B. His heart wouldn't stop beating hard in his chest. Six months away from Rose had seemed to last forever—he didn't want to spend a minute longer away from her, and today he'd tell her. Tyler would fix things between them.

After reading the move-out email two months after Rose sent it, Tyler had panicked. Rose was leaving him. He'd almost jumped on the first plane for Boston to tell her to stop punishing him and come back home. Given the way she'd chosen to say goodbye to him, Tyler knew Rose wanted him as much as he wanted her. That last night together had been the only thing keeping him sane during all these months apart. Still, he'd decided to let her cool down while he was away. Once he got back, he was certain he could charm her into forgiving him.

Now the moment had finally arrived.

More than receiving Rose's forgiveness, Tyler simply wanted to be with her. No one, not one girl, had ever made him feel anything close to the passion he had for Rose. She was his best, and oldest friend; Rose was kind, smart, and smoking hot. All his fears of a serious commitment, however important they'd felt before, seemed irrelevant now. Rose mattered more. Being away from her had made Tyler realize just how much he needed her, how lost he was without her. *So much wasted time.*

Tyler pursed his lips. Yesterday had been the last lost day. Today he'd tell her he was in love with her, and everything would be fine.

He took a deep breath and rang Rose's doorbell. Quick, excited steps preceded the door opening.

"You're early," Rose said with a big smile. Then her eyes met his, and the smile disappeared, replaced by shock. A gasp escaped her. "Tyler."

"Surprise," he said uncertainly. Rose's dark eyes were different: they held a coldness Tyler wasn't used to. Well, he deserved it. He'd pulled a number on her, but he was sure he could make her forgive him. Especially with what he'd come to say. "Expecting someone else?"

"I didn't expect to find you on my doorstep," Rose said noncommittally. "Come on in. When did you get back?" She was still awkward, guarded.

"Last night."

"How was Paris? I was making coffee, you want some?"

Rose was nervous; she always busied her hands with something when she needed to calm.

"Coffee would be great, thanks," Tyler said. "Nice new place."

"Yeah, I was really lucky to find it." Rose avoided meeting his gaze as she spoke.

"I've brought you a housewarming gift and some upscale chocolate." Tyler handed her a gift-wrapped package and a Fauchon tin box.

"Fauchon, wow. Fancy." Rose set down the chocolate and unwrapped her present. "Thank you," she said, beaming. Her fond tone told Tyler he'd scored a point. "I've been looking for something red since I moved in," she added, still smiling as she admired the bright lacquered apple he'd bought in a Parisian design shop. "This house needed a splash of color."

Rose studied some options and finally positioned the apple in a corner of the kitchen island where it'd be visible from both the kitchen and living room.

"Wow, it looks perfect." Rose stared at him with a renewed light in her eyes. "Thank you."

This was his moment.

"Listen, Rose, I'm sorry." Tyler took her hands into his. "I've been an idiot and messed up badly. But everything happened so suddenly, so unexpectedly. I didn't know what to do, then there was France, and there wasn't much I could've done about that. Rose, I'm sorry. I've been a jerk, and you didn't deserve it. Can you forgive me?"

"Tyler, I forgave you a long time ago." Rose shook her head, sighing. "We made a mess. I wasn't such a straight arrow either, but that is all gone now. We're fine."

Tyler couldn't believe his luck. The reconciliation had been even easier than he'd expected. "I couldn't wait to see you, to say how sorry I am."

"Come on, cheer up. We're fine."

"I've missed you so much."

"It's okay now."

Rose leaned in for a hug, and Tyler shifted sideways to kiss her.

"Whoa!" Rose pushed him back, planting both of her hands on his chest. "I said we're fine, not 'let's make out.'"

"If we're fine, why can't we make out?" Tyler asked, leaning in again.

Rose wiggled away, putting space—and the kitchen island—between them. "You just said you were sorry, and the minute I say it's okay, you try to jump me?"

"What's wrong with jumping you? I want to be with you, Rose." Tyler tried to come around to her side of the island, but she made a stay-there gesture. Okay, he deserved some grief. But now he needed to make her see how much he cared about her. "These months away from you have been a nightmare. I was stupid before and scared about getting serious with you, but I had time to think, a lot of time, and I'm sure now. We can make it work. Please give me another chance."

"Tyler, no. We both know it won't work. We're great as friends, and that's it. Look at the mess we made last time. Let's be *just* friends. Please. I want my best friend back."

"And I'm here. But I want more. So what if it was messy last time? I've said I'm sorry. Why can't we try again?"

"Listen, Tyler." Rose braced her hands on the countertop. "I'm not saying it was all your fault because it wasn't. The mess was as much me as it was you. But now we've had enough time to cool off and we can go back to how things were before, like it never happened."

"But I can't pretend, and I don't want to. Rose, I've spent the last six months thinking about you, and only you. I don't want to be friends with you. I want everything—the whole package. I've never felt like this about anyone else."

"That's because you're my best friend, and we've known each other forever. Tyler, listen, please. We can't be anything more than friends, we just can't. It'd never work."

"I'd make it work. I can't go back..." Tyler paused. "Rose, I love you. I'm in love with you."

Nineteen

Rose

Rose stared at Tyler, shell-shocked. She'd dreamt of hearing those exact words for over a decade now. Tyler, in love with her. A dream come true. Only reality didn't feel as right as the dreams. Thinking about it, she hadn't daydreamed about being with Tyler for some time, her heart had been somewhere else. A flash of blue eyes invaded her mind. Ethan's eyes. Georgiana's eyes. Rose sobered up at once.

"How did Georgiana take the news?" Rose asked, crossing her arms over her chest.

"Georgiana?" Tyler seemed dumbfounded. "What does Georgiana have to do with any of this?"

"I'm just curious. After all the strings she pulled to organize your romantic gateway in France, she must've been pretty stone-faced when you dumped her."

Tyler stared back at her in confusion.

"You *did* dump her, didn't you?" Rose pressed.

The dark shadow that passed over his face was enough of an answer.

"This is exactly why it'll never work," Rose said, turning away.

"Rose, if this is about Georgiana, don't worry. I can break up with her in a second."

"So why haven't you already?"

"Rose, it would've been awkward. We were in Paris, living in the same house—"

"And did you sleep with her while you were in Paris, living in the same house?"

Again, she could read the answer on his face.

"It didn't m—"

"Don't say it didn't mean anything."

Tyler stood silent, petrified in the middle of the living room.

"But Rose, I didn't cheat on you. It's not like we were together. If you give me a chance, I would—"

"It doesn't matter if we were together or not, don't you see?" Rose could hardly keep it together. Tyler's declaration of love had thrown her off, and now he was making her so angry. Rose didn't like how worked up she was getting. "You say you're in love with me. You say you've spent six months thinking about me nonstop. But that didn't stop you from sleeping with your girlfriend, and that's the problem."

"But we weren't together," Tyler protested.

"It's irrelevant. Love should be enough for you not to want to fool around with whoever else is available." Rose's voice trembled. "You shouldn't want to sleep with other people if you're in love with me. Period."

"You're not being fair. Why can't you give me another chance?"

"Because if you blew it, then we'd be over for good, and I don't want that. Plus…" Rose hesitated just for a moment. "I'm kind of seeing someone else."

"Who?" Tyler was suddenly cold.

"Ethan."

The name took a moment to register, and Rose witnessed the shock in Tyler's eyes when it did.

"Georgiana's brother?" Tyler hissed. "Are you kidding me? He's a bigger player than I am."

"He's not, at least not with me."

Tyler snorted. "Why does he get a chance and I don't?" His tone was bitter.

"Because if I break up with him, it's just that: a breakup. If we broke up, I'd lose my best friend too, and I don't want that to happen. Ever."

"It's not fair." Tyler pouted. "I would never hurt you, Rose, you have to believe that."

"Tyler." Rose moved closer to him. "I do. I know you wouldn't hurt me on purpose. And I know you think you can behave, but the fact remains... you probably wouldn't. There's too much at stake, and I care about you too much. Tyler, if you cheated on me, I would never recover from that. *Never.* And I'm not willing to take that risk. Plus, I'm happy with Ethan. Really happy."

At that, Tyler moved away and started pacing around the living room like a caged lion. "Bullshit, Rose. You care about me too much! If I tell you I can do something, it means I can. It's all about that dude, isn't it? Georgiana's brother was all over you from the moment he set eyes on you." Tyler sagged on the couch like an empty sack. "Do you love him?"

The question made Rose's legs unsteady. Did she love Ethan? She wasn't sure, but if it wasn't love, her emotions were something close enough. Rose sat next to Tyler, staring hypnotized at his legs twitching up and down. "Tyler... I honestly don't know."

He looked at her with sadness in his eyes. "I always thought we'd end up together at some point. I never thought I'd blow it so big time, or that I'd be too late."

Rose didn't know what to say to that. She'd felt the same for a long time. Even when she was with Marcus, somehow she'd sensed the relationship wouldn't last forever. But something had changed between her and Tyler. Rose had had a taste of what her love life with him could turn into. The paranoia, the jealousy, the second-guessing. She hadn't liked it, and it had made her not like Tyler that much either. Rose didn't want to not like Tyler; she loved him too much. But Rose didn't know if she was in love with him anymore, or if she'd ever been truly.

A long silence lingered between them.

Tyler spoke first. "Am I?"

"What?"

"Too late?"

Rose closed her eyes to search within herself and decide where she stood. She'd imagined Tyler saying all the things he'd just said to her a million times before. But in all her fantasies she'd been elated, giddy, out-of-this-world happy, and never… *empty*.

"Tyler, it wasn't meant to be between us. Not romantically. Even if I was willing to risk our friendship and give it a shot—which I'm not—the truth is I don't want to. I'm with Ethan, and I want to be with him. Can we go back to being just friends?" As she asked the question, she felt a bit hypocritical. If she had to be honest, they'd never been just friends. There'd always been something deeper between them—a deeper bond that the sex had ruined. She hoped with all her heart they could find a way back to each other, but she was no longer sure it was possible.

Tyler stood up from the couch without saying a word. He moved toward the door, opened it, and paused, his back to her. After a few seconds, Tyler stepped outside, slamming the door behind him, not once turning around.

Twenty

Ethan

Ethan drummed his fingers on the leather wheel of his black Mercedes as he waited for the light to turn green. Another red light, and Ethan swore he'd speed through it. The drive through town toward Rose's apartment was taking ages. Georgiana had just called him to say she was back, that she'd left France two weeks early to be with Vicky, and help her with her final wedding preparations. As happy as Ethan was to have Gigi back home, he was more scared of the three-hundred pound gorilla she'd brought along—Tyler Bronfman.

Boston felt too small for the two of them, and Ethan didn't like the idea of Tyler anywhere near Rose. After four months with her, Ethan was in a good place. But now the d-bag was back and Tyler and Rose would see each other every day at school, and possibly outside of it, too.

The notion irked Ethan in a way he wasn't prepared to handle. He'd known he was in trouble the night he and Rose met. Rose stirred something in him; she held a power over him that not even

Sabrina had had. Ethan wasn't the jealous type, but with Rose, he'd become possessive in a way he was ready to admit wasn't normal. And Tyler's return spiked this urge to new heights.

Finally, Ethan parked outside Rose's building and jogged inside, not stopping until he was standing in front of her door. When Rose answered, she had puffy eyes.

"Have you been crying?" Ethan asked, entering the apartment. "What happened?"

At once, he noticed a vivid red apple on the kitchen island. He didn't like the new addition. The thing was too red, too in-your-face, offensive almost. Ethan liked it even less than Rose's miserable expression, although he wasn't sure why. Not until he noticed the Fauchon chocolate box next to the apple.

"Nothing, I'm okay," Rose said.

"Found your red thingy?" Ethan asked, aware of the edge in his voice.

"Mmm, yeah, it's a present," Rose replied warily.

"From Paris?"

Rose nodded.

"How did Tyler know you were looking for something red?" Ethan asked between gritted teeth. "I thought you two weren't talking."

"We weren't, but Tyler knows me."

That was an even worse explanation, and Ethan lashed out. "Not twenty-four hours in the country and he's already been here? What did he want?"

"Ethan, please don't get jealous. I've had a bad enough morning already."

"Why? What happened?" Ethan's hands curled into fists and his knuckles went white. But he was mostly able to stay in control, and he resisted the desire to punch the wall as he listened to Rose's tale.

Rose

Ethan didn't look good. Rose had wanted to tell him everything, but looking at the cold fury mounting on her boyfriend's face right now, she wasn't sure she'd made the right choice. His jaw was set tight and twitching, while his hands were turned into fists, clenched so hard the knuckles were turning stark white.

"So let me get this straight," Ethan hissed. "The only reason you're not with Tyler is because you're too scared he'd break your heart. Otherwise, you would've already run off into the sunset together."

"Ethan, that's not what I said." Panic flared in Rose's chest.

"I must've gone deaf, then, because that's exactly what I heard."

Ethan and Rose glared at each other from opposite sides of the room, neither able to talk. Both were panting as if they'd just run a marathon.

"Ethan, please." Rose broke first. "Can you calm down? I don't want to argue with you. I'm just trying to be honest. Can we talk about it without shouting or getting mad?"

Rose watched him struggle to keep cool— Ethan was clearly beyond mad at this point. He flared his nostrils, paced around the room a couple of times, and finally settled on a stool at the kitchen bar. Rose was actually surprised by how quickly he'd calmed down—for the first time, she appreciated what it meant to be with someone older, more mature. Ethan might be mad, but he wasn't out of control.

"I'm listening," he said. "But I hate the power Tyler still has over you."

"Ethan, it's impossible not to be affected. If Sabrina walked through that door right now, you'd be upset even if you haven't seen her in five years. We're humans, not robots."

"I'm not in love with Sabrina," Ethan said pointedly.

"And I'm not in love with Tyler."

"Are you sure about that?"

"Listen, I care about him, and I always will. But no, I'm not in love with Tyler. I'm not sure I ever was."

Ethan's shoulders relaxed.

"The nerve of that dude," he grumbled. "He still hasn't broken up with my sister, and he came here to get all over you. Makes me want to punch him."

"Please don't. I'm happy with you, and I don't need anyone else. But Tyler is still a big part of my life."

Ethan shrugged, annoyed.

"I know you don't like our friendship," Rose pressed, "but can you accept it?"

Ethan was silent for a few tension-charged minutes, making Rose wonder what was going on inside his head. Finally, he looked up and pinned her with a hard stare.

"Talk to me," Rose whispered.

"I've been in this situation before." Ethan shook his head. "With Sabrina, I'd noticed one stare too many between her and Max, but I didn't trust my instincts. I couldn't believe what was right before my eyes. I didn't want to. And I ended up being made the fool. I won't make the same mistake twice.

"Rose, I trust you, so I'll ask you one last time: Are you sure Tyler is just a friend to you? After everything that happened? And please, be honest. I couldn't stand walking in on you and him together. So if you're not one hundred percent sure, if you need time to think things through, just say so. I'd much rather we end things now, clean. If you say there's nothing between you two, you have to mean it."

Ethan's speech was so full of passion it made Rose's tingle all over. Her body practically sang with warmth.

"Ethan, I do mean it," she said. Rose closed the distance between them and cupped his face in her hands. She didn't need to think about it, she was sure. "I want to be with you. Only you." Rose leaned in and kissed him.

He tugged her into a bone-crushing hug that told Rose how scared he'd been over possibly losing her. She smiled.

"I prefer you when you smile," Ethan said.

"I prefer you when you're kissing me."

"Ah, Miss Atwood, I must oblige you then." He kissed her again. And after breaking the kiss, he added, "What do you say we make it official?"

"How?"

"My sister, Vicky, is getting married in two months. She's been pestering me to know if I'm going alone or with a date. Would you like to be my plus one?"

"Whoa! And meet the entire Smithson clan, are you sure?"

"As I'll ever be. I promise they don't bite."

Rose hesitated, and Ethan stiffened in her arms.

"I mean, if you don't want to, I completely understand. You don't have to come. I can go alone."

"No, I want to… but…"

Ethan raised his brows.

"Will Georgiana be okay with me coming? I mean, I don't want to create an awkward situation at your sister's wedding. Everyone in your family should be relaxed and able to enjoy the day, Georgiana included. If she still hates me…"

"As long as she's with Tyler, I don't see why she should have a problem."

"You think Georgiana will go with Tyler?"

"She already told Vicky she would."

"And don't you think that's going to be even more awkward?"

"To be honest, I don't care. Georgiana is my sister, and you are you. If we stay together, you girls will have to learn how to talk to each other while keeping your claws sheathed. And I want you to meet my family."

"I don't have claws," Rose protested.

"You sure?"

"Mm-hmm."

"So you're coming?"

"I guess so. I mean, it's only a day. How bad can it be?"

"Oh. I should've said the wedding is on Martha's Vineyard... for the entire spring break."

"You bastard."

"I'm sure you can survive."

"Isn't the middle of March too early to go to Martha's Vineyard?"

"What can I say, my family is weird. And Vicky loves the island at the end of winter."

"How can a wedding last for *a week*?"

"I've no idea." Ethan tucked her in closer to him, and Rose felt reassured that with him by her side, she could endure an entire week of Georgiana. And maybe after France, Georgiana didn't hate her so much. Rose could only hope.

Twenty-one

Georgiana

Georgiana pulled on a hairband to keep her hair out of her face. "Can I use your concealer?" she asked Vicky.

They were doing their makeup in Vicky's hotel room on Martha's Vineyard. The same way they used to when they were younger and both lived with their parents. A giant mirror lined the upper half of a wall with a cozy shelf underneath that now resembled a beauty booth. Downlights in the ceiling completed the setup, making it better than a professional dressing room.

"Use this one," Vicky said, passing her a stick with a built-in brush. "It's the best."

Georgiana and her sister shared the same pale complexion, dark hair, and sparkly blue eyes. Same as Ethan, same as their father when he was younger, before stress and age turned his hair to white.

Georgiana flicked the brush all around her eyes and while she waited for her skin to absorb the liquid concealer, she turned in her chair to look at Vicky.

"What do you think of the stray?" she asked.

On their second night on the island, after a day of studying Rose and Tyler interact, Georgiana wanted a second opinion.

"Come on, Gigi," Victoria said. "Rose isn't a stray. She seems perfectly nice to me."

"She's a sneaky little ho. I can't believe Ethan brought her here, and that he dumped Alice for that bitch."

"Who's Alice?"

"One of my best friends and my sorority little sister," Georgiana explained. "You met at Christmas, the year before last. Madison's friend who came to the house?"

"Yeah, I remember her."

"Anyway, Alice was dating Ethan when Rose stole him. That's what she does."

"I don't know. What if Ethan was over your friend? After Sabrina, he's gone through so many girlfriends."

"Exactly. So why stick to the stray? He must be out of his mind."

"He seems a little out of his mind," Victoria agreed. "But in a Sabrina-out-of-his-mind way."

Georgiana lowered the sponge she was using to apply foundation and threw her sister an evil glare through the mirror. "You think he's in love with her?"

"Gigi, you're blind if you haven't noticed."

"I hoped he wouldn't be so stupid."

"Why? I haven't seen Ethan this cheerful in years. You should be happy for him."

"I would be if it was anyone *but her*."

"Didn't you ask him to go out with her a while ago?"

"Yeah, but only because he usually chews girls up and spits them out in the blink of an eye. I never thought he'd be so dumb as to actually fall for her. And that was before he was dating Alice, anyway."

Before her sister could reply, there was a knock at the door. Only one eye done, Vicky closed the mascara stick she was using and went to answer.

"Hi," Madison, their younger cousin, said.

"What are you doing here?" Georgiana asked.

"I invited her." Vicky gave her a pointed, be-good stare in the mirror.

Madison blushed. "If you were talking, I can come back later."

Geez. Her cousin was such a pushover Georgiana almost didn't enjoy teasing her. It was too easy.

"Actually, yeah," Georgiana said. "We were having a private conversation. So if you don't mind…" She made a shoo gesture.

Madison was already turning toward the door when Vicky stopped her. "Don't be silly, Madison." Victoria took Madison's hand and made her sit in front of the giant mirror. "We were only discussing Ethan's new girlfriend."

"Rose? She seems really nice."

"Of course you'd think that," Georgiana snapped.

Madison blushed again and lowered her gaze. While their cousin wasn't watching, Vicky slapped the back of Georgiana's head and mouthed, "Stop it," in the mirror. Aloud, she added, "I like her too."

Madison lifted her head and gave a weak smile. "I preferred Alice, though."

Vicky's eyes widened, making the lack of mascara in one even more obvious. "What's so special about this Alice?" she asked Madison.

"She's my roommate and best friend," Madison confirmed. "It would've been super cool if she'd joined the family. Anyway, she has a new boyfriend now, so all's well that ends well…"

Georgiana rolled her eyes. "Quoting Shakespeare, Madison? Seriously?" She wondered how Alice could live with her cousin without shooting herself in the head. Madison was so boring. "Here." Georgiana passed Madison the liquid concealer. "Start with those awful circles under your eyes. You spend too much time locked inside, reading poems."

Madison made a grimace in the mirror but did as she was told.

Georgiana finished smudging eye shadow on her lids before she said, "Anyway, you're both wrong. Rose is a horrible person."

Vicky sighed, exasperated. "What is it you have against her?"

"For one, as soon as her ex dumped her, she was all over Tyler. Even though he was with me, she moved into his house right away and who knows what else she tried to do."

"Rose and Tyler seem pretty cold towards each other," Vicky said, finally applying a thick coat of mascara on the missing lashes.

"That's true," Madison said. "They barely spoke last night at dinner."

"Which only proves my point," Georgiana continued. "Why did they argue? Probably because he's with me and not with her."

"I don't know." Vicky shook her head. "To be honest, I don't like the way Tyler glowers at our brother every time they cross paths."

"What are you saying?"

"Just be careful," Victoria said. "I don't want you to get hurt."

"So you think the stray is still after Tyler?"

"*Enough.*" Vicky banged a hand on the shelf, making the makeup items bounce. "Stop calling her that. Or, at least, don't let Ethan catch you."

"All right, I'll call her by her full name, then, *Rosalynn*." Georgiana smirked. "How quaint."

Vicky rolled her eyes. "Anyway, to answer your question: no. From the way she looks at our brother, she's not after Tyler. Are you sure it's not Tyler who's after her?"

Georgiana positively glowered at Vicky and noticed Madison shrink in her chair.

"Excuse me," Georgiana hissed. "You're talking about my boyfriend. Tyler wouldn't be with me if he was into her. We're perfect for each other, and who knows? Maybe in a year's time, it will be me getting ready for my rehearsal dinner."

Or sooner, if her new plan worked. France had not been the success she'd hoped for. They had had a lovely time in Paris, with no arguments or troubles. But their relationship lately could be summed up as lukewarm. Tyler was slipping away from her. And even if she'd never admit it aloud, she suspected Tyler still wasn't out of reach from Rose's claws. So, at least for now, she tolerated Ethan's relationship with her, as it provided a sort of safeguard. But with a bit of luck, soon there'd be no doubts about whom Tyler belonged to. And Georgiana was confident Ethan would grow tired of Rose sooner or later. She couldn't wait for the time she'd be rid of the stray for good.

Twenty-two

Rose

Rose shuffled around the dining hall of the hotel, hating that Ethan was not by her side for this social apéritif. But her boyfriend had a lot of friends on the island who he hadn't seen in months, and Rose couldn't demand he babysit her every second of the week. Still, she found it hard to socialize with so many unknown people. Not to mention she was on edge trying to avoid both Tyler and Georgiana. The wedding party was a certified minefield.

On cue, Tyler walked into the room, and Rose navigated the other guests to disappear into the adjoining hall. Too busy with her escape to pay attention to other people, Rose bumped into someone.

"Oh, I'm sorry," she said.

"Please don't be. You must be the famous Rose," a distinguished man with trimmed white hair said. "I'm Ethan's father, Bradley Smithson. Nice to meet you."

"Rosalynn Atwood. Very pleased to meet you, sir."

"The pleasure is all mine. It isn't often that our boy brings home a girl. Ethan tells me you're in your second year at Harvard Law. Have you already decided what branch of the law you want to follow?"

"I'd like to work in litigation in the area of criminal law, sir."

"Oh, interesting." Mr. Smithson chuckled. "I have a soft spot for criminal law myself. Many interesting cases. In fact, a couple of years ago we had this case on our hands..."

Mr. Smithson started outlining the grounds of the case, and Rose listened attentively. Was he putting her to the test? He must be. Why else would he discuss legal matters with her five seconds after introducing himself? Ethan's dad finished his speech and stared expectantly. "What's your legal opinion?" he asked.

Yes, *definitely a test.*

Rose collected her thoughts. In the particular case he'd outlined, textbook solutions would only get the defendant into deeper trouble, which was probably why he'd selected it. So what would a shrewd lawyer do? Was there a way out? Some aspect was escaping her. She concentrated, trying to get a firmer grasp on the solution. After closing her eyes for a second, inspiration hit. *Jurisdiction!* It was a jurisdiction issue. The crime had been committed on a federal enclave and it did not fall within the jurisdiction of the state where it was being tried. Her dad had told her about a similar case ages ago.

Rose smiled and offered her response.

Mr. Smithson smiled back, a new respect twinkling in his eyes. "Do they teach that to second year students these days?"

"No, I don't think so. But my dad has always been passionate about the law. As a child, he read me supreme court sentences instead of fairy tales."

"Hi Dad," Ethan said, coming up from behind them. He stepped up next to Rose and slid an arm around her waist in a protective gesture.

"Son," Mr. Smithson said, acknowledging Ethan with a nod. Then he returned his focus to Rose. "Your father is a lawyer? I'm not aware of any Atwood law firms in the Boston area."

"Oh, no. He couldn't pursue a career. When my grandparents died in a car accident, he'd barely finished college before he had to go back to Dallas to take care of his younger brother and sister."

"Dallas? What does your father do back in Texas?"

"He's in real estate."

Ethan tightened his grip on her waist, he clearly tensed at the mention of his profession in front of his father, even if they were discussing her dad's work and not Ethan's.

"Atwood, Atwood," Mr. Smithson repeated. "Are you by any chance related to David Atwood?"

"Yes... he's my dad," Rose replied, embarrassed.

Mr. Smithson's eyes bulged for a brief second before he caught himself.

"Well, I'll let you young kids enjoy the party," he said. "It was a real pleasure meeting you, Rose." He smiled fleetingly, then turned on his heel and was gone.

Ethan

Ethan followed the exchange between Rose and his father with unease. Since he'd started his own business, his relationship with his dad had been hard, to put it nicely. To say his dad could barely stand to look at him would be more accurate. Smithson and Smithson was the number one law firm in Boston. And for one of "the heirs" to abandon it was a slight too serious for his father to ever forgive.

Ethan wouldn't have put it past him to make a sour remark to Rose, making her uncomfortable just to get at him. Even if, so far, they seemed to get along well. Yet when Rose mentioned her father was in real estate, Ethan was ready to go on the offensive if his dad dared say something insulting about that particular line of work.

Instead, his dad had stunned him by recognizing Rose's father by name and winking at him just before he'd left. Bradley Smithson—w*inking*! Dad had shown no comradeship toward him since, well, since he'd abandoned the law. What was up with him? Ethan looked at Rose, perplexed, and was even more confused when he found her blushing tomato red.

"What was that about?" he asked.

"Not now." She looked mortified. "I'll explain later."

"Rose, is something wrong? Did my dad say something to you?"

"No, Ethan." Rose shook her head. "Your dad was perfectly nice."

"What then? Why did my dad know your father by name?"

"Can we do this later? I need a drink." She skipped forward, away from him and toward the bar.

Ethan followed, curiosity building. He wasn't going to let this go. He'd ask her later, in private, when he had better ways of mollifying her.

Twenty-three

Tyler

Tyler paced around his room, he was hiding from Georgiana and still hadn't managed to speak to Rose. How had things come to this? He was trapped in a relationship he didn't want, but somehow needed. The only reason he remained with Georgiana, ironically, was to be closer to Rose. Like this weeklong wedding—he'd agreed to come only because Rose would be here. Tyler had hoped he'd be able to talk to Rose, but Ethan stuck to her like a shadow. At least everyone was staying in separate rooms. Georgiana's parents were old-fashioned like that.

He picked up the room's phone and dialed nine.

"Reception, how may I help you?"

"Hi, hello, I'm here with the Smithson wedding party. May I have the room number of a guest?"

"Sure, sir. What's the guest's name?"

"Rosalynn Atwood."

"Miss Atwood is staying in room 2405. You want me to connect you, sir?"

"No, that's all, thank you." Tyler hung up.

Damn. Room 2405 was on the same floor as Georgiana's room, but he had to try. Tyler ruffled his hair in the mirror—yeah, the bad boy look suited him—and walked out of his room.

After waiting for what felt like hours for the elevator to arrive, Tyler hopped in and pushed the second floor button. To his relief, there wasn't a soul in the hallway on the next floor. So why the anxiety? He wasn't doing anything wrong. And if someone caught him… ah hell, America was still a free country, wasn't it?

2401, 2403… there, room 2405. The door had a bell, but Tyler decided to knock since he didn't want to risk someone from an adjoining room hearing the bell ringing. When no one answered after a minute or so, Tyler knocked again. Was Rose not in her room? Was she still downstairs in the dining hall? That wasn't likely—when he'd left the party, Tyler had searched for her. Rose wasn't downstairs. Rage seared his veins. Was she in Ethan's room? Tyler knocked once more, louder this time, so that if Rose was inside, it would be impossible not to hear.

"I think you have the wrong room," a deep voice said from behind, making Tyler jump. "My sister is two doors down the hall."

Tyler turned around to meet a stare of manly hate. Ethan had a black expression that told Tyler the dude was more than ready to fight. He wouldn't mind knocking out the old guy, but instincts suggested the move wouldn't score him any points with Rose. The two men stared at each other aggressively for a few seconds, until Tyler finally broke eye contact and moved down the hall without saying anything.

He paused at Georgiana's door and looked back before knocking. Tyler watched Ethan go through the door that had remained shut for him, and a wave of resentment took over. He rapped his knuckles on Georgiana's door in a loud, vindictive knock. Not that Rose cared about anything—or anyone—he did anymore.

The knowledge made him livid.

Rose

When Rose heard the first knock, she assumed it was Ethan. Only her innate sixth sense prompted her to have a look through the peephole before throwing the door open. Seeing Tyler standing in the hall outside froze her cold. What did he want? Rose couldn't go through another conversation like the one they'd had in January. Not here, not now. Even if they'd hardly spoken in a month and a half, it was too soon. Their friendship was still bleeding from a thousand wounds, and they couldn't afford to add more fresh cuts. Plus, Ethan was going to be here at any minute, and the three of them standing in a confined space together was a hell-no situation.

Even through the glass's distortion, she could see Tyler's pained expression, and it killed her. She backed away from the door. Rose couldn't bear to see Tyler suffering like this. But what could she do? Nothing Rose could say right now would improve the situation—it'd only make it worse. The easiest thing was to pretend she wasn't in her room. If she didn't open the door, Tyler would go away, and they'd talk another time. Yes, this was the only sensible thing to do. But as another knock came, and then another, her heart churned. Rose willed Tyler to leave because it wasn't in her nature to shove him away, over and over.

"I think you have the wrong room."

Ethan's voice sent a chill down her spine, and Rose glued her eye to the peephole.

Ethan and Tyler were glaring at each other like angry beasts ready to attack.

"My sister is two doors down the hall," Ethan added, his tone as cold and hard as metal.

Tyler's expression was murderous—not that Ethan's was all hearts and clouds. If Rose could magically dematerialize right now, she would. Her heart beat faster as the two stood there, glowering at each other. After what seemed like forever, Tyler finally left.

A soft knock came immediately after, and she opened the door to let Ethan in. His stare was a wall of ice.

"What did he want?" Ethan hissed.

"I don't know."

"I don't like it, Rose. I don't like it one bit." Ethan nervously paced around the room. "I don't care if he's a big part of your life or your best friend; if he keeps this shit going, I'm going to whack the bastard."

"Ethan, calm down. Everyone's going to hear you if you—"

"I don't give a shit if everybody hears."

"But your sister—"

"It'd be about time she opened her eyes. Listen, Rose, I have to tell her. I can't stand that he's all over you while he's still dating her."

"Tell her what, exactly?" Rose said icily.

"About you and Tyler. Your history together. I have to tell her. It's the only way she'll be able to move on."

"Ethan, you can't tell her that. When I told you, you said I wasn't talking to Georgiana's brother."

"But she's obsessed with him, how else can I make her see the truth?"

"Not by telling her about me and Tyler. You promised."

"I know, I know. But it's killing me to see the way he's hurting her. And I can't stand him anywhere near you." Ethan's shoulders relaxed for the first time since he came into the room.

"Come here." Rose grabbed his hand and pulled him toward the bed, where they cozied into each other's arms. "I know it's hard," she said, stroking his hair. "But I'm sure everything is going to be all right. Tyler and Georgiana will break up on their own. If Tyler doesn't love her, he'll break up with her. To be honest, I'm surprised he hasn't done it yet."

"What if he doesn't?"

"Ethan, I don't think he's going to propose to your sister, so they'll break up sooner or later. And when it comes to me... look, he's been spoiled his whole life. He's not used to hearing no. This is just a tantrum. It'll pass. He needs some time. That's all."

"I still don't like it."

"I know, and I'm sorry."

"Don't be. It's not your fault." Ethan kissed her forehead. "But don't think you're so easy to forget."

Rose scrunched her face.

"You're adorable." Ethan showered her face and neck with tender kisses. "You even impressed my dad. I told you he'd want to adopt you."

"Oh, come on. He was just being polite."

"No, he wasn't. Rose, he winked at me! You must've done something to really impress him. And why did he know your father?"

"About that." Rose flushed red. "Remember when I said my dad was in real estate?"

"Mm-hmm."

"I may have understated that a little. I mean…" Ethan looked at her questioningly. Rose hoped he wouldn't see her differently after she told him. "Let's just say his company is just shy of a Fortune 500…"

Ethan stared at her. "What, you're saying your dad's a real estate mogul, and you're a billionaire?"

"Pretty much." Rose's cheeks flared hot. She was sure her face was about to melt.

"That would explain my father's approval. If I'd known you were an heiress, I wouldn't have rented your place to you at half price."

"You said the owner didn't want to have it go to frat boys!"

"More the owner wanted to get in your pants."

"It's your apartment, isn't it? You sneak!"

"Me, sneak? What about all that 'I have a low budget' crap you pulled, Miss Heiress?"

"I prefer Miss Atwood. And my reasonable-rent need was true, I don't like to flaunt my dad's money around. I prefer to live on a reasonable budget until I can make a living of my own. And I don't like people knowing about my dad, because no matter what they say, they look at you differently once they find out."

"I know the feeling. It was the same in school for me. Once my surname was public knowledge, I had a whole lot of new *friends*. I hated it."

"So you get it?"

"I do."

"Are you mad I didn't tell you?"

"No." Ethan leaned in and kissed her.

"You must've really liked me to pull that rent stunt," Rose said with a mischievous smile. "How much did you lose?"

"I do a little more than like you. And I didn't lose anything. I gained you. Rose…" Ethan paused. He almost never used her first name, and it gave Rose goose bumps all over. "I love you."

Rose's heart skipped a beat. "I love you, too," she replied, one hundred percent sure of her feelings.

Tyler was forgotten. The man standing next to her consumed everything in Rose's world. Ethan, the man Rose loved and who loved her back. He kissed her and Rose sighed, forgetting everything, even her name.

Twenty-four

Rose

"Tyler?" Rose said into her phone. She'd heard nothing from him since the wedding two months back, and now he was calling her out of the blue.

"I-I need to talk to you." Tyler sounded agitated. "Can you meet me?"

"Right now?"

"Yeah, right now."

Rose looked at her watch. In forty-five minutes, she had a meeting for a group project that was due in less than a week. "I have a group meeting in forty-five minutes, but we can meet on campus and talk there before I head to the library to meet the others."

"Rose, to hell with classes and finals and group projects!" There was a hint of desperation in his words. "I need to talk to you, and it's going to take a lot longer than forty-five minutes."

"Tyler, did something happen? What is it?"

"Not over the phone. I'll pick you up at your house in fifteen."

The line went dead. Tyler had hung up without leaving her room to reply.

Exactly fifteen minutes later, her doorbell rang. Rose picked up her bag and hurried to meet Tyler downstairs at his car.

"Hey," she greeted him, opening the passenger door and climbing in. "What's up?"

Tyler turned toward her, and Rose gasped. With his ghastly pale skin, bloodshot eyes, disheveled hair, and dark, five-o'clock shadow, her best friend looked a mess. Thinner than she'd ever seen him, and ten years older.

"Tyler, what's going on?" Rose asked, alarmed.

"Later." He put the car into gear and started driving, gripping the wheel so tightly his knuckles turned stark white.

After ten minutes of driving in silence with no radio and no talking, Rose began to feel uneasy. She had no idea where they were going. They might be heading north, but that was the extent of Rose's sense of orientation.

"Tyler, can you at least give me a hint here?"

He shook his head. "I can't talk about it in the car… I can't…"

"Can I at least ask where we're going?"

"Salem."

Salem? Was this a witch-hunt? But when they kept going on I-93 North instead of turning onto I-95, Rose realized they were going to Salem,

New Hampshire, not Salem, Massachusetts. The "why" remained a mystery. She kept quiet for the rest of the ride until they stopped in the parking lot of what looked like an amusement park.

Why would Tyler want to drive forty-five minutes on a random Saturday to go to an amusement park? And on a day like this? At the end of April, the weather was still chilly and windy, and the park looked like a ghost town. Rose had so many questions she wanted to ask him, but once again, she didn't. Certain he wouldn't answer anyway, she decided to wait, even if Tyler looked more wretched with every passing minute.

She followed him to the ticket booth where he bought two daily passes. Tyler took a free map of the park and started walking down a paved path. Rose walked behind him, a million scenarios playing in her head. Was this about them, their friendship? Their love quadrangle? They hadn't talked properly after the wedding. When they bumped into each other on campus, there were always other people around to provide a buffer. The unspoken arrangement had suited both of them. Somehow, though, Rose knew this mysterious trip was about something else. Tensions lingered between them, but nothing strong enough to turn Tyler into the mess he appeared to be right now.

Rose was so absorbed in her thoughts, she didn't see Tyler stop, and when he did, she bumped into his back.

"We're here," he said.

Rose followed his gaze upwards and saw they'd stopped in front of a Ferris wheel. Her heart jumped in her throat. So it was something bad, really bad. Ferris wheels were their special place. The most important turning points of their life and friendship had been discussed while on a wheel ride. Mostly the one back at home, the Texas Star, but others worked in a pinch, too.

Rose thought back to some of the things they'd said and done inside a Ferris car. They'd promised each other they would be friends forever, piercing their index fingers with a needle and mixing their blood to seal the pact.

When they were twelve, they'd shared their first kiss—just because they'd decided they should practice the technique together before they did it for real with someone else. At least, that had been Rose's excuse. She'd wanted Tyler to be the first boy she kissed. It had also been on a Ferris wheel that Tyler had told Rose about losing his virginity. Years later, Rose had done the same.

On one dreadful ride, they'd tried their first beer out of a flask Tyler had stolen from his dad and hidden under his football jacket. The beer had been warm and disgusting, and Rose had ended up getting sick, earning them one of the harshest groundings in their teenage history.

They'd opened their Harvard admission letters together in a car much like the ones currently rotating high above her. After high school, they'd gone less often, but Rose had cried over Marcus for the first time while on a ride. They'd kept the tradition of going at least once whenever they were at home in Dallas.

Everything important had been said on a Ferris wheel, and now here they were in front of one. Tyler had something so big to tell her that it called for a wheel ride. What was it?

A cold shiver crawled up Rose's spine. She was scared.

"I know it's no Texas Star," Tyler said with a forced smile, "but it was the best I could find up here."

There was no line, and as they entered the first available car, an eerie silence lingered between them. As soon as the ride started, Tyler dropped his head into his hands, and Rose realized with horror that he was crying. She'd never seen Tyler cry. *Never.* Rose wanted to comfort him, but she didn't understand why he needed comforting. Asking didn't seem like an option, so she just sat beside him in sympathetic silence.

After the wheel did a full circle, the attendant on the ground moved forward as if to help them dismount, but Rose signaled they were taking another ride. The park was empty. No one was in line, and after their second go-round, the attendant left them alone and kept the ride spinning.

Cold air blew on them, especially when they passed the upper part of the wheel. Still, Rose buttoned her jacket to the neck and waited patiently for Tyler to be ready to talk, ignoring both the wind and the cold.

"My life is over," Tyler said once they reached the top for the third time. "I feel so sick I want to throw up."

"You're ill?" Rose's voice cracked.

Tyler shook his head.

"Tyler, what is it? Tell me." Rose felt ready to explode from anxiety.

"She… she's…" Tyler shook his head again. "She trapped me."

"Who? Who trapped you? What do you mean?"

"Georgiana."

Another chill raced down Rose's spine. "What did she do this time?" There were no more semesters abroad to force on him. "Is it school again?"

"No." Tyler kept shaking his head in his hands. "I'm done. No way out."

"Tyler, what did she do?" Rose whispered.

"She lied. S-she tricked me. She did it on purpose. She says she didn't, but I know she did."

"What? What did she do?"

Tyler let out a desperate cry. "She's pregnant."

Twenty-five

Rose

After his confession, Tyler cracked and collapsed into Rose's arms, crying like a baby. Rose hugged him close to her chest, whispering soothing words, all the while boiling inside with rage. Tyler was one hundred percent right. Georgiana had done it on purpose. Probably telling Tyler some lame excuse about the pill not always working or some other false crap. Rose didn't need to hear the details. When her phone started vibrating in her bag, she shifted in the booth to turn it off without looking at the caller ID.

"Pick up if you need to," Tyler half-sobbed.

"No. Whatever it is can wait." Rose let Tyler have a few more minutes. When he seemed a little calmer, she asked, "Have you... mmm... discussed options?"

"There's nothing to discuss. Georgiana says she wants to keep the baby."

Well, of course, after all the trouble the bitch went through to engineer the pregnancy in the first place. Rose felt homicidal. "And what do *you* want?"

"It doesn't matter what I want, I can't have it."
Tyler sighed. "Rose, I want my life back. I want
you back. But, most of all, I want our friendship
back!"

"Tyler, I'm here, and we're friends. No matter
what happens, we'll always be friends. I'm so
sorry Georgiana did this to you, but we'll get
through this pregnancy like everything else. What
are you going to do?"

"No clue." Tyler shook his head. "What *can* I
do?"

"Well, Georgiana didn't leave you much
choice…"

"She didn't leave me *any* choice. Even if she
was open to discussing options, you know my
views on abortion, and she knows them, too."

"How come?"

"She knows I'm adopted and against abortion,
as I wouldn't be here if my biological mom had
one."

"You told her you're adopted?" Rose was
shocked; Tyler never told anyone.

"Yeah."

"When?"

"Ages ago. I don't remember when. The topic
just came up somehow…"

"Oh, Tyler, look at me, please."

"What?"

"You'll be an amazing father for this baby, no matter what."

"Rose, please. I'm the most irresponsible person in the world. I can't take care of myself. How will I care for a helpless child?"

"That's crap and you know it. Tyler, you're a good guy, and you'll be a great dad."

"Stop saying that word. I want to throw up."

"And who said morning sickness was just for the girls?" Rose attempted a joke.

Tyler looked grim. "I'm going to be someone's father."

"It appears so."

Tyler and Rose sat in silence for another half-turn of the wheel, both staring at the view, lost in thought. Until Rose finally spoke. "I feel a bit guilty about this whole situation."

"Guilty, you? Why would *you* feel guilty?"

"Do you think Georgiana would've gone to these extremes if I hadn't moved in with you? It made her go cuckoo jealous."

"I don't care if Georgiana was jealous—she didn't have the right to do this to me. When she told me…" Tyler growled. "All I can say for myself is that I didn't strangle her—and not because I didn't want to."

"Ethan says she's obsessed with you—"

160

"Don't bring *him* into this discussion," Tyler hissed. "I don't want to remember he even exists right now. And please don't tell me again I should've dumped Georgiana a long time ago. I don't need an 'I told you so' speech. I'm already aware of the mistakes I've made. Don't you think I regret every day not leaving Georgiana right after we... Anyway, I think about it every day. If I had, we'd be together now, and you wouldn't be dating the devil's brother, and I wouldn't be having a baby *with* the devil!"

"Don't go there. This is not your fault."

"But it is, Rose, it's all my fault. If I hadn't been so damn scared, right now we'd be happy together. I've been an idiot, Rose. I wanted to be with you so bad, but I was scared because I knew with you, it would've been the real deal. And so I did what I do best: I ran. I ruined everything. Georgiana got all scheme-y because I left her suspicions room to grow. I shouldn't have stayed with her, I shouldn't have gone to France, and I should've used a condom even if Georgiana swore she was on the pill. I mean, how many idiots have been in my position before?"

"Listen—I'm not condoning what Georgiana did because it's so wrong on so many levels. But it shows you how much she cares about you..."

Tyler snorted.

"In her own perverse way, I think Georgiana really loves you. Look at all she's done to be with you. And it's not like she's after money or anything." In the past, Rose had suspected more than a few of Tyler's girlfriends of finding his wallet more attractive than the person. Georgiana wasn't one of them. "The Smithsons are well off, so all Georgiana has to gain from this mess is you, and I'm not saying you should forgive her—"

"Are you sure? Because that sounded a lot as if you were making excuses for her."

"No, there's no excuse for her behavior. But I am stating a fact: Georgiana loves you. A lot."

"Love?" Tyler scoffed bitterly. "You don't trap the people you love."

"True. Let's say her love leans a little toward the selfish side—okay, a lot toward the selfish side—but you can't deny it's there. What about you? How do you feel about her?"

"I hate her, Rose. I *hate* her." Tyler stared ahead at empty space. "Don't even make me think about her…"

"Tyler…"

"I don't like that tone."

"Can I ask you something?"

"I have a feeling you're going to ask anyway."

"How did you feel about Georgiana—I mean, really—before all this happened? Before… me?"

Rose gripped the security metal bar. "Were you in love with her? Because if I have to be completely honest with you, she used to scare me more than any of your other girlfriends. And that's why maybe... er..."

Tyler turned toward her with a confused frown. "What are you saying, Rose?"

"I'm saying that before I messed things up, you seemed really happy with Georgiana. I'm saying that partially—*subconsciously*—things may have happened between us when they did because I felt threatened by Georgiana. Yeah, I was sad about Marcus, but I was also jealous of you and Georgiana." Rose released a breath. "Oh, Tyler. I've been selfish and stupid and petty. I couldn't stand her, and I was scared she would take you away from me for good. That's part of the reason we—I mean... did... you know... when we did."

"If you felt that way, why did you turn me down when I came home begging to be with you?"

"When you moved to France I had time to clear my head. I know I love you, and I thought I was in love with you for most of my life... but then all that shit happened, and you moved to Paris, and then... I met Ethan, and..."

"Please don't tell me how much you're in love with him because I couldn't stand to hear it right now."

"That's not… My point is this: I idealized you for more than a decade, and you probably did the same with me. In my head, I'd always pictured us ending up married after you straightened up a bit and had seen enough women naked to be good for life…"

"Yeah, I had that same idea. But what's your point?"

"My point is that maybe this fantasy we've both been having was just that—a fantasy. What I'm saying is, in all the years I've known you, I've never seen you as emotionally involved as you were with Georgiana. I mean, before I spoiled everything by jumping into bed with you because I wanted to ruin your relationship. Because if I'm being honest, that's what I wanted. I couldn't stand that you hadn't cheated on her. I couldn't stand that you were no longer making a go at me, so I had to go ahead and screw your love life."

Tyler smirked. "Quite literally."

Rose blushed but smiled. This was the first glimmer that made her recognize the Tyler she loved under the broken man, under all his sadness and worries. If Tyler could make jokes on a day like this, there was still hope.

"To be honest," Rose continued. "I've been the worst friend—person, even. Worse than Julia

Roberts in My Best Friend's Wedding. I am the fungus growing on pond scum."

"No, you're just the scum," Tyler said with the tiniest hint of a smile. "We both are. But Georgiana… she's the fungus feeding on scum."

"She's a bit of a fungus or the mucus of the fungus… But the fact remains that despite everything—despite me, and France—you didn't break up with her. It has to mean something."

"I came to that stupid wedding only because I wanted to see you."

"Okay, but you had a million other opportunities to dump her, and you never did."

"I've already told you, I'm aware of all the mistakes I've made. I don't need you to rub my face in them."

"What if it wasn't a mistake? You've never been faithful to someone for as long as Georgiana. Before I ruined everything, I mean. Not even with Jessica. So, are you sure you can't find that love again, that there's no way you could ever forgive Georgiana and be happy with her? Even if she's a bit… mmm—"

"Of a conniving bitch?"

"I was going to say *pushy*. I know you're mad right now—"

"Mad doesn't begin to cover it."

"Okay, but the only choice you can make right now is how to fit into this baby's life."

"Meaning?"

"Meaning: are you going to be a single dad, or are you and Georgiana going to be a family?"

Twenty-six

Ethan

Ethan had been pacing up and down Rose's lobby for an hour now, and his patience was running thin. Why wasn't she picking up the phone? She was with him, wasn't she? The notion only served to fuel his anger. He had the keys to Rose's apartment, being the owner, but it didn't feel right to let himself in when Rose wasn't there. She hadn't given him a key, and anyway, waiting inside the apartment would hardly be better. At least down here he'd see Rose the minute she came home.

Half an hour later, Ethan watched a black car pull up in front of Rose's building. *Tyler's car.* So he'd been right, they were together!

The lights of the car went dark, and everything stood still. If Rose didn't come out of that damn car at once, Ethan would not feel responsible for his actions. He wanted to snap Tyler's neck so badly, and his being in the same car with Rose did nothing to calm the urge.

Luckily, just when Ethan was about to spring into action, the car lights came back on and Rose climbed out. As she trotted up the few steps to the front door, the car sped away.

Rose's eyes widened as she entered the lobby and spotted him. "Ethan?"

"Why didn't you pick up your phone?" Ethan accused, not even bothering with a hello.

Rose fired a question back instead. "Did you talk to Georgiana?"

Ethan nodded.

"So do you really need to ask why I wasn't picking up the phone?" Ethan was about to come out with some petty retort, but Rose cut him off. "Listen, it's been a long day. Why don't we go upstairs to talk?"

He followed her to the elevator, and as it climbed to her floor, both kept quiet. The metallic ding announcing they'd reached Rose's floor sounded deafening after their silent ride.

"I want pizza, a giant one," Rose said, unlocking the door and taking off her jacket.

"Pizza? How can you think about pizza right now?"

"I skipped lunch, I'm hungry, and I could use some comfort food. Are you mad at me for some reason?"

"You were with him all day, don't deny it. And you didn't pick up your phone!"

"If you're up to date on the 'good' news, I don't really need to explain why I spent the day with Tyler. He's still my best friend, and I'm his. Tyler needed to talk to someone. Do you want just cheese or pepperoni?"

"Just cheese," Ethan said, pouting.

Rose dialed the delivery number. "Um, hello. Yes, one cheese pizza and one pepperoni, please... Rose Atwood... correct, that's me... okay, perfect. Bye." She hung up and opened the fridge. "Beer?"

"Yeah, I need one before I go strangle that bastard." Ethan flopped onto the couch.

Rose handed Ethan his beer and sat rigidly next to him. "Excuse me?"

"You heard me."

"Yes, I did, but honestly, this whole situation is hardly Tyler's fault."

"Last time I checked, it took two to make a baby."

"Yes, it does take two, but if one of the two says she's on the pill when, in fact, she's not... all it takes is one lying b—"

"Watch it," Ethan threatened. "You're talking about my sister."

"I don't care if she's your sister. You're not on Georgiana's side on this, are you?"

"I'm not even sure what her side would be. Her side would be Georgiana not being pregnant with that bastard's baby, and her never seeing Tyler again."

"Well, that'd be Tyler's side, too, but it's too late for that."

"And whose fault is that?" Ethan looked at Rose pointedly.

"Are you saying it's my fault? How is any of this my fault?"

"If you'd let me talk to her, tell Gigi the truth, she would've never done it."

Rose glowered at him, eyes black with anger. "Don't you even dare go there," she hissed. "There's no way it's my fault if your psycho of a sister decided to get herself pregnant. *No. Way.* So don't even try to put this on me. Why are *you* mad, anyway? The only person with any right to be angry here is Tyler."

"Of course you'd be on darling Tyler's side."

"You're being petty on purpose. Are you mad because I spent the day with him? Is this only a jealousy tantrum?"

"Rose, I can't stand him. And you spent the entire day with him not picking up your phone."

"Because we were talking. There weren't any romantic implications in the conversation. Tyler is destroyed... I've never seen him this bad."

"He's a cheating, lying—"

"And what does that make your sister?" Rose continued to glare at him. "Georgiana schemed and lied just as bad."

"At least Gigi did it for love. Why did he do it? Why did he stay with her if he doesn't love her? Only to be closer to you, or to make you jealous, and now my sister will pay the consequences for life."

"Only because she got herself pregnant against Tyler's will. And please don't act as if you were a beacon of moral behavior. None of us have been."

"Meaning?"

"How many casual hook ups did you have after Sabrina?"

"Don't try to turn the focus away from that bastard—"

"Really? Georgiana traps him and Tyler is the bastard?" Rose was close to screaming.

"Calm down," Ethan said.

"No, you calm down." Rose shot up from the couch. "You haven't answered me."

"What was the question?"

"How many girls have you screwed without being in love?"

Ethan shrugged. "A few," he said casually, seeking to hurt Rose, to infuriate her.

It worked. Her nostrils flared in anger, and Rose struggled to keep her voice steady as she spoke. "Tell me, Ethan. How would you have felt if one of those girls had trapped you by deliberately lying about taking the pill? Think about it." Rose gave him a minute to, before continuing. "What if Alice had played the same trick on you? Would you be rooting for her, saying how, after all, you were the bastard for not loving her? I don't think so."

Touché. He was no saint, and neither was Georgiana. Ethan began to calm down. Rose was right; he was being over-protective of his sister, and over-jealous of Rose's relationship with Tyler.

"I know you love your sister," Rose continued, "and that you're worried about her. But for once, this mess was not Tyler's fault, or mine. It was all Georgiana. One hundred percent her. She's far from stupid or naïve, and she knew all the risks and consequences when she decided to go through with her little scheme. So it's all on her."

"But she doesn't know about you and Tyler. Maybe if she'd known, she wouldn't have done it."

"Didn't you say Georgiana suspected us? Do you really think it would've stopped her, even if she knew for sure? Seems like the opposite to me. It would've made her even more desperate to cling onto Tyler, instead of stopping her altogether."

"Maybe you're right, but what if you're wrong? I need to tell her. Please, let me tell her."

"Why? What good would it do now?"

"She could reconsider and…" Ethan didn't like what he was about to say, but he saw no other solution. "Not have the baby."

"Tyler would never let her do that."

"Why not? It'd be the perfect way out for him."

The doorbell rang in the background.

"Pizza's here."

Rose buzzed the delivery guy in. A few minutes later, she was back on the couch with two huge cardboard boxes and two more beers. They ate the first half of the pizza in silence. Ethan didn't want to be mad at Rose, but he was. He was convinced that if she'd let him talk with Georgiana, none of this would've happened.

"Why do you think Tyler wouldn't let her end the pregnancy?" Ethan asked.

"Because…" She looked unsure and wiped her mouth on a napkin to cover. "Well, you'll find out anyway sooner or later. Tyler is adopted and against abortion."

"Really?"

"Mm-hmm."

"Does Georgiana know?"

"She does, has for a long time."

Ethan snorted. His sister really was a piece of work.

"Do you think that's part of the reason she did it? Because she knew Tyler would want to keep the baby?"

"I'm pretty sure she took everything into account."

"Dooming herself for life."

"And bringing Tyler along for the ride."

"What is he going to do?" Ethan wasn't able to keep the animosity from his voice.

"What would you do in his place, since you seem to have all the right answers today, Mr. Self-righteous?" Rose sounded hurt more than angry.

Her vulnerability made him feel ashamed. He'd been yelling at her all night for no reason. Ethan had wanted someone to blame, but he shouldn't target Rose.

"Come here," Ethan said, grabbing her by the waist and pulling her onto his lap.

"Oh, so I'm back to hugging privileges?"

"And kissing privileges, too…" It felt good having her close, kissing her. Ethan relaxed. "It's just that my sister is crazy, and I can't stand him. But I'm sorry I took it out on you."

"Well, you'd better get used to Tyler being around; he might become your brother-in-law soon."

"Ugh, don't say that."

"Why?"

"Do you really think he'll propose?"

"They'll either split up for good and be single parents, or they'll get married and give it a shot at being a family. And, despite what you think, Tyler has a pretty big sense of responsibility, especially when it comes to family."

"Has he already decided?"

"No, but I think he'll try. At least if he can start looking at Georgiana again without wanting to kill her on the spot. It'll take time... but eventually, once he has come to terms with the situation and the idea of becoming a father..."

"But is that the best option?" The prospect of Georgiana marrying Tyler made Ethan sick. "Will he keep being a cheating loser if they get married?"

"I don't have a crystal ball. I've no idea what's best or how it will turn out. All I know is that Tyler will love this baby with all he has. He'll be a wonderful dad; I'm not so sure about a great husband. It's hard for anyone to start a family and have kids, but if you're forced into it, especially if you're Tyler..." Rose shook her head.

"So my sister basically dug her own grave."

"It's not necessarily going to be a fairy tale wedding, but there's a part of Tyler that cares about your sister. If he can forgive her, they could make it work."

"At least Mom will be ecstatic if she has another daughter married before the end of the year. And my dad too, with all these lawyer genes getting mixed up. He'll have a lawyer empire with all these grandkids."

"Mmm… but with us, babies could end up with mixed real estate genes…" Rose blushed all of a sudden. "Not that… I mean… I wasn't saying we should have kids or anything, it was just… you know…"

"You're so cute when you blush."

"And you're so annoying when you look that smug."

"That's not true; you adore me all the same." Ethan smirked. "So much so that you want to have my babies."

"I-I said it just for the sake of talking."

Ethan pressed one hand to his chest mockingly. "Now you're hurting me."

"Oh, stop it."

She silenced him with a kiss, and he wasn't about to complain.

"I have to study," Rose said after a short make-up cuddle. "Finals are in ten days, and I haven't done any homework today. Plus, I have a bunch of angry emails from my group project members who I blew off at the library that I need to read and reply to. Do you mind spending a cozy night in while I study?"

"I couldn't imagine a better way of spending the night than cozied in with you, and I always have work to do."

"I love you," Rose said out of the blue. "Never doubt that."

"I love you too, Miss Atwood." Guilt still gnawed at him, though. He'd been too harsh with her today. Rose didn't deserve to be treated this way. "Sorry again for today. I know it's not your fault. I was as worried for my sister as I was mad you spent the day with Tyler."

"You know," she said, and kissed Ethan, "the feminist movement will shoot me for saying this, but I sort of like it when you get crazy jealous. You're annoying as hell but way too adorable."

"I won't tell, I promise."

Rose got her books from her room and sat at the dining table. Ethan sat next to her, took out his iPad, and they began working and studying, respectively. Despite all that was happening, Ethan found himself happier than ever. A simple night in, doing ordinary, boring stuff, and Ethan was in heaven because he had Rose by his side.

Twenty-seven

Rose

"Woo–hoo! Finals are over!" Rose tilted her face up, enjoying the first warm day of May.

"You mind taking a walk with me?" Tyler asked seriously.

"Is Georgiana around?" Rose checked behind them.

Since the pregnancy announcement, Georgiana had become even more clingy and possessive of Tyler. Which usually resulted in escalating nasty behaviors toward Rose.

"Nah, she had an exam right"—Tyler checked his watch—"about now. We should be good for at least two hours."

"Okay then."

They walked in silence until Tyler stopped in front of a sunlit bench. He sat on the backrest and Rose sat on the bench next to him, her head level with his knees.

"So, I might've decided what to do with Georgiana and the baby," Tyler announced. "But I need to talk to you first."

"Okay…" Rose's heart started beating faster.

"I'll ask her to marry me and try to make it work. But before I do, I need to know you mean it when you say there isn't a future for us. That you see me as just a friend."

Air left Rose's lungs. So this was the moment when she'd have to say goodbye to Tyler forever. The day had been coming—fast—but somehow in all the scenarios Rose had imagined, being on a bench in the sun on campus had not been one of them.

Rose's voice failed her, the words caught in her throat. She paused and tried again. "Tyler, I don't see you just as a friend. You're so much more than that. You're my best friend, my oldest friend… you're family, and I love you."

"But you're not in love with me anymore."

Rose shook her head.

"'Cause you love him."

Rose nodded. Funny how Tyler and Ethan kept avoiding saying each other's names and just kept calling each other *him.*

"I hate his guts, you know."

"If it's any consolation, Ethan hates yours, too."

Tyler snorted. "Excuse me if I don't feel sorry for him."

Rose tried to keep her emotions in check. Her relationship—um, friendship?—with Tyler wouldn't be the same after today. For years, they'd flirted with the possibility of romance, of a distant future together. But today they were putting a stop to that for good. Rose hoped she'd manage to finish this conversation without bursting into tears.

"Okay, then. I'll be a married man soon!"

"You already guessed what I would say?"

"Pretty much."

"How?"

"From the way you look at him; you've never looked at me that way. Rose, you've never looked at anyone that way."

"Can I get a hug?" Rose was about to break down.

"Course you can. Come here."

Tyler jumped down from the bench backrest and pulled Rose into a tight embrace. A new sadness overcame her, and hugging Tyler provided little in the way of comfort. This newfound melancholy would take a long time to shake off. But, at least for the first time in forever, there wasn't tension between them.

"Promise me we will stay best friends no matter what happens," Rose whispered.

"Hey, I know I've gone soft, but I'm not Paris Hilton BFF material yet." Tyler smiled. "And who knows? You could become my sister-in-law very soon. One day, we'll be one big, happy family!" he added sarcastically.

"Aw, come on." Rose pushed him away and sat back on the bench. "It's not like I'm going to marry Ethan anytime soon."

"If he's not stupid, he'll ask you. Plus, he's such an old guy; he'd better get a move on."

Rose beamed at Tyler. It was good that he was making jokes again.

"So, when are you going to propose?" she asked.

"This weekend," Tyler said, sitting next to her. "Just before the term ends. Knowing Georgiana, she'll want to get married straight away before her bump shows."

"You've already picked a ring?"

"I have one on hold…"

"You seem calm enough."

"No. I'm freaking out, Rose. My guts are screaming at me to hop on a plane, go get lost somewhere in Asia, and not come back for years. But, like you said, I'll become a father no matter what, so I want to at least try to be a decent one."

"You'll be a great dad, Tyler. I'm sure of it."

"I have another question for you…"

"Is this one easier?"

"Pretty straightforward. Will you be my best man?"

"Of course I will, Tyler!"

"Thank you. It means a lot to have you there by my side."

"Will Georgiana… mmm… be okay with me being your best man?"

"Why? You think she has you lined up for the maid of honor role?"

"Ha, ha. I'd be surprised if she let me inside the church at all."

"Between me and the old guy, I'm sure she won't have much of a choice."

"He's not old!"

"He so is. So, will you be there by my side?"

"Always!" Rose squeezed his hand. They'd been on a long journey that had seen them together and apart, but, finally, Rose had her best friend back.

Twenty-eight

Rose

A mere three weeks later, Rose examined Tyler's appearance in his wedding suit. They were in the chapel's side room reserved for the groom, and the ceremony was supposed to start in one hour. After Tyler's proposal, Georgiana had not wasted a second. The Bronfman-Smithson wedding had been organized in record time.

"You look like a ghost," Rose said.

"And you look like a boy."

"I was under strict orders to dress in a tux and comb my hair in a low chignon. Your wife-to-be was worried I'd ruin the visual equilibrium of the ceremony if I were to stay by your side dressed like a girl."

"What?"

"Interpreting Georgiana's thoughts with some liberty, I think she wanted me to look as ugly as possible."

"You're never ugly, not even when you dress like a boy."

"Well, I wasn't forbidden from wearing makeup at least. How are you doing?"

"I want to throw up."

"That good, huh?"

"Yep. Where did you leave the old guy?"

"Ethan's outside helping his father welcome the guests. Your parents are doing the same. It's a funny mix… You can spot the Texans from a mile away, even if they can't wear hats inside the church!"

"Bet you can." Tyler chuckled. "How was the big dinner last night?"

"I suspect my mom has a crush on Ethan. As for my dad, he couldn't understand how someone could not want to be a lawyer, but he and Ethan had plenty of topics to discuss, and they hit it off pretty well…"

"Uh-huh."

"You asked," Rose said, straightening his bowtie.

"I'm a masochist, didn't you know? Why else would I be doing this right now?"

"Because you're a good man, because it's the right thing to do, and because despite what you might think, deep down you care about Georgiana. A lot. And, I had a little peek at the bride; she's going to take your breath away," Rose said, smiling.

She was trying her best, but seeing Tyler marrying someone else wasn't the piece of cake she'd expected. Seeing Georgiana resplendent in her white gown hadn't helped, either.

There was a knock on the door. Ethan came in.

"How's everything going? Gigi wanted me to check that everything was in order... You're a little on the pale side," Ethan added, looking at Tyler.

A gasp caught in Rose's throat. Ethan in a tux was something else. She was melancholic about Tyler and everything, they had a lot of history that was hard to let go of, but *Ethan* was her future. Of this, Rose was certain.

"You try the 'getting married' thing, and then we'll see how you look," Tyler retorted.

The two men still didn't like each other. But they were coming to terms with the fact that, for better or for worse—literally—they were about to become family.

"You sound like my mother now! Anyway, I come bearing gifts." Ethan removed a flash and three plastic shot glasses from his jacket. "Here," he said, filling each with a transparent liquid and then passing them out. "To the bride and groom—cheers!"

The three of them raised the glasses, tilted their head backwards, and downed the shot in one swig. Rose wrinkled her nose—blech, vodka. A little too strong for the a.m. hours, yet Tyler looked far happier than he had a minute ago. There was even some color returning to his cheeks.

"If we're all set, I'll go tell the priest we can start," Ethan said, tucking the flask and glasses back into his jacket. "You should come out in a few minutes and wait for the bride at the altar."

Tyler nodded bravely.

When Ethan was gone, Tyler turned to Rose. "The old guy… he's not too bad."

"I know." Rose was close to tears again. Vodka was a great idea for a guy with a bad case of cold feet, but probably not the best for an overemotional friend.

"Come here," Tyler said.

Rose went over to him and they hugged tightly. This felt like the last private moment they would ever share.

"Nothing will change between us," he whispered in her ear.

"Nothing," she said, repeating the lie.

Tyler let go of her. "Let's go do this," he said. He straightened his jacket and then marched out of the room.

Rose watched him go, knowing that in many ways she was letting go of him, forever. When she came out of the small room, she was just Rose—there was no more Tyler and Rose.

***

"I'm not sure if the fact that I find you hot while you're dressed like a boy should scare me or not," Ethan teased as he and Rose waltzed across the dance floor—a platform that had been set up in the middle of the Smithson's family home garden.

"I'm about to cut into your dilemma," Rose said. "Do you think the style-gestapo will flay me if I let my hair loose? This chignon is killing me. And the bow tie is strangling! How do you guys wear these around your neck every day?" She started pulling some pins out of her hair.

"Here, let me help…" Ethan pulled her to the edge of the garden and started working his fingers into her hair.

When the last pin came loose, Rose shook her head and let her hair cascade down onto her shoulders. Ethan was already undoing the bow tie.

"I have to stop now, or I'll end up undressing you completely. It wouldn't be very proper."

"No, it wouldn't, especially not with your mother staring at us. She's been watching us like a hawk all day. What's up with her?"

"Ah, my dear." Ethan grinned. "I'm afraid that with my sister's nuptials, I remain the sole Smithson sibling yet to be matched. I'm pretty sure my mother has designs on you."

"Aren't two weddings in six months enough for her?"

"Is the thought of joining yourself to me in holy matrimony so unappealing to you, Miss Atwood?"

"What? No, I-I mean…" Rose was stuttering, her face searing red. "Are you serious?"

"Why not?"

His stare was like burning ice.

"I thought you w-were against getting married."

"I'm against girls shopping for rings after one date; I'm not against getting married to the woman I love."

"Are you proposing?" Rose's heart was beating way too fast.

"Now, don't go getting a big head, Miss Atwood…"

She swatted him playfully. "Jerk."

He grabbed her hand and pulled her into a kiss.

"I love you," Ethan whispered. "One day, I want you to be my wife. What do you say?"

"One day." Rose couldn't help but smile like an idiot. "I love you too."

"Now that my noble intentions are in the open, can I bring you to my room?"

Ethan and Rose discreetly disappeared behind a bush and ran across the lawn toward the house, holding hands and laughing like a pair of kids. Never, not even in her wildest dreams, could Rose have imagined the day Tyler married another woman would end up being the happiest of her life. But life held many happy surprises in store, and running free on the grass holding the hand of the man she loved, Rose felt exactly that. The happiest she'd ever been.

To Be Continued

Note from the Author

Dear Reader,

I hope you enjoyed *Let's Be Just Friends*. If you loved my story, **please leave a review** on Goodreads, your favorite retailer's website, or wherever you like to post reviews (your blog, your Facebook wall, your bedroom wall, in a text to your best friend...). Reviews are the biggest gift you can give to an author, and word of mouth is the most powerful means of book discovery. It helps readers find new authors to love and it helps the authors *you* love stand out.

If you'd like to discover what happens next to Rose and Tyler, and if you'd like to meet new exciting characters, keep reading for a short teaser from the second novel in the *Just Friends* series, *Friend Zone*.

Thank you for your support and happy reading!

Camilla, x

Friend Zone Excerpt

One

Rose

Now

Inside the Smithson's country house, Rose followed Ethan up the stairs and down a corridor with too many white doors to count. He stopped in front of one toward the end, pausing with his hand on the handle. "You're about to have a glimpse into my teenage lifestyle," he said, and flung open the door.

Sprawled on Ethan's bed was a bulging middle-aged man, fast asleep and snoring.

"Rose, meet Uncle Frank."

Rose giggled, taking in what she could of Ethan's room before he closed the door. As it clicked shut, they tiptoed away, careful not to wake the sleeping man.

"We'll have to take one of the guest rooms." Ethan turned on his heel and headed back toward the beginning of the hall.

He opened a random door. Before Rose could get a peek inside, a roar of rage escaped his lips and he rushed into the room. Rose made to follow him but stopped dead on the threshold. She raised a hand to cover her mouth as she stared at the scene before her eyes in shocked silence…

Two

Alice

Seven Months Ago

Jack had beaten her to the library. He was waiting in the small reading room, head bent over his laptop and a cute frown on his face. He hadn't spotted her yet, so Alice paused and studied him through the glass door.

Even seated, it was easy to tell Jack was tall; all basketball players had to be. Not to mention playing varsity sports gave him a lean, flat-muscled body all too visible under his tight T-shirt and faded jeans. Dark eyes and hair, high cheekbones, and a straight nose made her best friend dangerously gorgeous. And his mouth... it was made to keep girls awake at night, which unfortunately it did—*too often.*

As Alice leaned closer to the glass, a dark lock slipped out from behind her ear, startling her. She still wasn't used to being a brunette. What would Jack say? Would he like it? Only one way to find out. Alice grasped the door handle and her chest tightened. He would reject her. Telling Jack the truth now was a bad idea; she should wait. *Yeah, definitely wait.* Today was a regular work-on-your-group-project-and-not-tell-Jack-you-love-him day.

Alice pushed the door open. "Hey," she greeted Jack.

"Hey, Ice." Jack looked up from behind his laptop. "Whoa!" His dark eyes widened in shock, and his gaze made Alice's stomach flip. "What's up with the hair?"

"Change of style." She dropped her messenger bag on the floor and sat in the chair next to him. "Ethan dumped me." Alice pretended the news was trivial as she set up her laptop on the table.

"So you dyed your hair black?" Jack tousled his fringe, perplexed.

It was a habit of his, one that made Alice want to run a hand through his soft curls every time he messed them around. The gesture exposed more of his biceps, too, making Alice wonder what kissing him would feel like if she were free to lock one hand in Jack's hair, pull his lips to hers and wrap the other hand around the marble-like smoothness of his arm.

She mentally slapped away her hands, and said, "I was tired of the fake blonde. Like it?"

Alice hoped the makeover would stir something in Jack, but he ignored her question point-blank.

"What happened with the dude? You've been dating him for what… three, four months now?"

"Remember when I told you about the night of Georgiana's birthday party?"

"Your former sorority big sister?"

"A big sister is for life, even if she graduates and moves on to grad school. But, yes, her."

"She's hot." Jack smirked. "You should introduce me."

"Can't do. She's in Paris with her boyfriend until next semester." Alice rolled her eyes, and Jack laughed.

"So? What does Georgiana have to do with Ethan dumping you?"

"Well, he's her brother, for one—"

"Seriously?" Jack made a mind-blown gesture.

"Yeah. We were at that hip sushi restaurant downtown for Georgiana's birthday and Ethan ditched me at the table to go flirt with this other girl. But then he showed up at my place later and apologized, and I thought we were okay. It was business as usual—and then he ghosted me for a month straight."

"That's awful."

Jack was clearly trying and failing to keep his lips from twitching. Ghosting was his favorite breakup strategy.

Alice ignored his distracting lips, and said, "The radio silence was driving me mad, so last night I confronted him. He didn't even try to deny it."

"The ghosting part, or that he's seeing someone else?"

"Either. Both," Alice admitted. "At least he was honest."

"Do we know *the other woman*?"

"No, but she's a grad student, too."

"Hot?"

"Yeah, she's hot." Alice swatted him playfully. "You're not helping…"

Jack waggled his eyebrows. "Want me to seduce her for you?"

Yeah. Just what I need. "I doubt she's into college juniors."

"You never know," Jack said, focusing on his laptop screen. With a few clicks of the mouse, he opened the 3D model of a complex molecule they had to design for their Organic Chemistry group assignment. Jack started to rotate the model but stopped to regard Alice with a suspicious air. "Wait, is this girl… What's her name?"

"Rose."

"How sweet," Jack said. "Is she a brunette?"

Alice's cheeks burned. "Yep."

"Hence the hair change?"

"No. Ethan made it clear I got a one-way ticket to the dumpster. Dark brown is actually my natural hair color. I've decided I want to be truer to myself from now on. Starting with my hair, I guess." *And my feelings for you.*

"If it's any consolation." Jack knocked twice on the table. "Lori and I are over, too."

A melting started in her stomach. Jack's low voice did weird things to her. Especially when he was saying he was single. Alice had feared Lori would become a long-term problem. And now, *poof*, she was gone. Was it a sign she should talk to Jack today? And say what? I love you? *Nah*, maybe a physical approach would be better with Jack. She should just grab his face and kiss that mouth. *How will he react if I do that?* The thought made her cheeks flame red, and Alice decided to take it slow. She didn't have to kiss him right now. Better to hear about the breakup first.

Alice pursed her lips, schooling her face to appear concerned instead of elated as she spoke. "Why? I thought your bio major was a keeper, what with all her talk of med school and her short skirts."

Jack snorted. "Until she went from super fun to a clingy nightmare in the space of five dates."

"I wasn't the only one who had a bad night, huh?" Alice suppressed a satisfied smile. Her plan to make a move on Jack had just become much simpler.

"Mine was horrible, trust me."

"Worse than mine? At least you did the dumping." Jack hated confrontations, in particular with the girls he dated. Hence the ghosting. "What happened? Lori a crier?"

Jack scowled at her. "It's not funny. She's a kidnapper. Batshit crazy."

"A kidnapper?" This was a new one. "What did she do?" Alice was genuinely curious at this point.

"She picked me up after school because we had a date." Jack abandoned the 3D model and turned toward Alice. "So I naively got into her car."

"Wait—to dump her?"

"Yeah, my plan was to tell her and leave."

"Wow, no ghosting?"

"Nah." He shook his head. "I'd run into her too often to pull that off. She's taking pre-med Chemistry, remember?"

"No, I'd forgotten," Alice lied, and gestured for him to keep talking.

"So I got into her car and she drove away. I asked her if we could go talk somewhere quiet, and she told me I'd just read her mind."

"She was expecting the 'Sayonara' speech?"

"No way. This is where my tale gets interesting." Jack grimaced as if in pain. "I noticed she was heading out of town toward the middle of nowhere, so I asked her where we were going. 'A special place,' she told me."

"Oh gosh." Alice put a hand to her head. "This story is about to get dreadful, isn't it?"

"In a second. The best part is coming." Jack winced. "I tried to tell her I didn't have much time, and that we needed to talk. She ignored me and kept driving, insisting I had to see this place, no matter how many times I asked her to pull over."

"But couldn't you make it clear you didn't want to go?"

"Believe me, I did. At that point, I had two options: either keep sitting in the car, or grab the wheel and make her pull over by force." Jack frowned at the memory. "Lori literally kidnapped me."

"How long were you in the car?"

"Close to an hour?"

Alice let out a low whistle. "Where to?"

"This is the worst part." Jack groaned. "She took me to this scenic viewpoint on top of a hill and timed it so we would get there at sunset."

Alice almost felt sorry for Lori, except that her total fiasco served Alice's cause too well.

"My day is improving," she said. "Now I can cross myself off the most-humiliated-girl spot. What happened when she stopped the car?"

"I tried to speak first, but she wouldn't let me."

"Of course not." Alice chuckled. "What did she say?"

"She told me she was falling for me, that I was the only guy she'd cared about in a while…" Jack paused. "Her speech ended with the L-word."

"Oh gosh, poor girl. And that's when you told her?"

"Yep."

"And what did she do?"

"Let me just say the one-hour drive back to the city was… *awkward*." Jack sing-songed "awkward."

"Well, at least she didn't leave you stranded on the hilltop." Alice's mouth trembled with the effort of not smiling. "I would have."

"Nah, Lori might still hope she can change my mind."

Alice's pulse sped up as she asked, "Can she?"

"No way. If I had any doubts, yesterday's trip cleared them up for good." Jack made a gun with his fingers and shot himself in the head. "Worst Friday night of my life."

"Really?" Alice couldn't hide her amusement.

He nodded. "Really. Ice, why don't you turn on your laptop and we get going. You can give me more grief later. Deal?" Jack added a stomach-flipping wink.

"Deal," Alice whispered, suddenly out of breath.

As she powered on her Mac, her fingers prickled with optimism. Both their relationships had ended on the same day; it had to mean something. Today *was* tell-your-best-friend-you-love-him day. She'd wait until they were done with the project to speak to Jack. *Or jump him.* He was single and wouldn't stay so for long; this was her moment. After all, how bad could it go? Not as tragic as with Lori. The worst he could say was no...

Acknowledgments

Thank you to all my friends. To Ladan in particular for having me as a guest in her house in Boston for ten days. I fell in love with the city and the Harvard campus during that time and I wanted one of my stories to take place there.

For the first edition. Thank you to my editor Michelle Proulx, to my proofreader Emily Ladouceur, and to my beta readers.

For the second edition. Thank you to my editor Hayley Stone.

Finally, thanks to you for your continuous support.

CPSIA information can be obtained
at www.ICGtesting.com
Printed in the USA
BVHW03s1221280618
520316BV00003B/120/P